THE BOOK OF THE BANSHEE

ANNE FINE

Resource Material
Rachel O'Neill

Series Consultant
Cecily O'Neill

Collins Educational
An Imprint of HarperCollins*Publishers*

Published by Collins Educational
77–85 Fulham Palace Road, London W6 8JB
An imprint of HarperCollins*Publishers*

First published 1995

ISBN 000 330310 1

Acknowledgements
The following permissions to reproduce material are gratefully
acknowledged:
Illustrations: cover illustration from *The Book of the Banshee* (the
novel) by Anne Fine, Puffin Books, 1993, © Caroline Binch, p. 56;
Hulton Deutsch Collection, pp. 72, 74, 76, 84; The Illustrated
London News Picture Library, p. 73; Imperial War Museum, p. 80;
Sally and Richard Greenhill, pp. 86, 87.

Text extracts: from *The Book of the Banshee* (the novel) by Anne Fine,
first published by Hamish Hamilton Ltd, published by Puffin Books,
1993, pp. 56–58, 62, 68; from *Hideous Kinky* by Esther Freud,
Hamish Hamilton Ltd, 1992, p. 66–67; from *The Children We
Deserve* by Rosalind Miles, HarperCollins*Publishers* Ltd, 1994,
extrapolated from *Families and How to Survive Them* by Robin
Skynner and John Cleese, Mandarin, 1983, p. 68; from *The Roses of
No Man's Land* by Lyn Macdonald, Michael Joseph Ltd, 1980, pp.
74–75; from *On the Beach at Cambridge* by Adrian Mitchell, Allison
& Busby, 1984, p. 77; from *Hack* by Ed Harriman, Zed Books Ltd,
1987, pp. 78–79; from *How High the Moon, Boann and Other Poems*
by Susan Connolly and Catherine Phil MacCarthy, Poetry Ireland,
1991, pp. 82–84.

Design by Wendi Watson
Cover design by Chi Leung
Cover photograph by Mark Kensett (Innes Studios)

Commissioning Editor: Domenica de Rosa
Editor: Helen Clark
Production: Susan Cashin

Typeset by Harper Phototypesetters Ltd, Northampton
Printed and bound by Scotprint Ltd, Musselburgh

CONTENTS

BACKGROUND
TO THE PLAY

Authors are always being asked, 'Do you write about people
you know?' and, as Jan Mark has pointed out, they mostly
can answer in all honesty: 'No. I write what I know about
people.' The idea for 'The Book of the Banshee' came when I
realised that the last dozen times I'd been out with friends,
we'd spent the whole time discussing our teenage offspring.
'You won't **believe** what Sam did last week.' 'That's nothing.
Wait till you hear what Tanya said to me yesterday.' On and
on and on.

And 'on and on and on' was at the root of it all. The sheer
exhaustion of the daily battles about mess, or loud music, or
what time they were to be in. Those with experience said
the worst of it was usually over in five years. Some parents
were reduced to duty shifts. '**You** tell her she can't go out
looking like that. It's your turn. I spoke to her this morning
about doing more homework.' From all around came reports
of explosions, and tales of senseless destruction. 'Hair dye
on **everything**!' 'Sat on the radiator. Naturally, it fell
straight off the wall.' 'Wore it for three days and it looked
like a rag.'

Meantime, I was reading the most extraordinary book. In
1937, no doubt distressed by the coming shadow of war,
Thomas Suthren Hope published 'The Winding Road
Unfolds', an account of his time in the trenches twenty years
earlier. The book was dedicated 'to the volunteers under
military age of all the belligerent countries who served
1914–1918'. Sadly long out of print, this is the finest
soldier's account of the experience of the First World War
that I've ever read. It's hard for an author to say why he or
she chooses to combine disparate themes in a book. Battles
at home and abroad may mirror each other in many ways;
but in sheer gravity, they're clearly not comparable. That

war in particular will never be a subject for flippancy. So the challenge of the original novel was to show where the similarities lay, and yet somehow neither drag down the humour of the warring teenage sections, nor trivialise the horrors of the Great War.

By making Will Fairway the mouthpiece of the novel, the technical problem was solved. Like everyone else his age, Will has a total range of response. He is capable of extreme levity and extreme sensitivity. His moods mesh and move naturally from one to another, and all are sincere.

There's **always** more in a book. More depth, more detail, richer characters and better and more frequent jokes. I'd **always** send the reader off to the library to track down the original novel. But in turning 'The Book of the Banshee' into a play, it was possible to preserve some of the balance between Will's obsession with the astonishing memoirs he's reading of a boy of his own age, and the more mundane but more immediate horrors of home life. Will's an 'Impeccable War Reporter', and he comes to understand that there are two forms of courage: the courage to endure, and, sometimes, the courage to refuse. Many of my American friends refused to fight in Vietnam. Many of the people I've worked alongside on political causes have had conscientious objections to war. It's a stance I respect, and, as the national response to conscientious objectors has shown over and over again, one that can take more courage and endurance than a mere falling-in.

In the novel, I tried to show how that sort of primacy of conscience can develop in someone like Estelle, the 'banshee' of the story. Free-thinking is frequently inconvenient to everyone around the free-thinker. The parents show the other form of courage – dutiful endurance in the face of exhaustion and the grim unknown.

In teenage, the simple authority figures of childhood lose their power. New patterns must develop. A long-settled childhood personality can fragment into tears and moods and sulks and rows and daft (and sometimes dangerous) behaviour. Out of the shards grows someone, not only larger, but usually more impressive. I tried to show how that new person can be well worth waiting for, and how, on the way, it can be a comfort and enlightenment to all life's combatants to find the circumstances of their lives mirrored in so many ways in so many good books.

Anne Fine

THE CHARACTERS

WILL – A thoughtful, bookish boy, halfway through secondary school. He is fond of both his sisters, though he's having a really hard time with the older one –

ESTELLE – Who is one year younger. However, she seems much more grown-up than Will, especially in her rebellious style of dress, and her sheer lippiness in the house.

MUFFY – Is their very young sister. She hangs on to her fairy-tale books the way other children cling to security blankets. She can talk, but she's fallen into the habit of avoiding doing so.

MUM – Heather Fairway is a busy solicitor. She's overworked and impatient, and anyone who looks at Heather hard enough can see where Estelle gets her grit and determination.

DAD – George Fairway is a tired garage manager. Gentle by nature, he tries to stave off trouble as long as he can, but he's learned from experience when to turn round and face it.

CHOPPER – Rupert M. Chopperly is Will's best friend. A neighbour, he comes round every morning before school. He's not bookish like Will, but he has a native intelligence that often carries him further faster.

THE BOOK OF THE BANSHEE

ACT ONE

Most scenes take place in the Fairways' kitchen, master bedroom or garden. One scene takes place on the way to school. The kitchen contains a fridge, cupboards, chairs, and a table covered by a tablecloth. It has a window and a door giving onto the garden and another door leading into the house. In the garden we see the kitchen window, a rabbit pen and hutch, a gate and an upturned wheelbarrow. There are some scales and a bed with a duvet in Mum and Dad's bedroom, which has a door and a window. A hedge and lamppost feature in the scene set on the street on the way to school.

SCENE ONE

In the kitchen. **Dad***, dressed but still yawning, is making tea.* **Muffy** *is dressed for school, and is spooning up cornflakes.* **Will***, in school uniform, and holding a book, is trailing round after his father.*

WILL   Dad! I need some lunch money.

DAD   My wallet's upstairs, Will.

WILL   I already **asked** you, upstairs.

DAD   When?

WILL   Before you got out of bed.

DAD   Well, I was asleep then, wasn't I? Stands to reason. In bed. Asleep.

WILL   You said you thought you had a bit of cash downstairs.

DAD   Out of the way, lad.

WILL   Dad! I need money for lunch. I need proper food. I had a piccalilli sandwich yesterday. The day before that, I had to have mint sauce on crackers.

DAD   Go up and ask your mother.

WILL   I've asked her twice. She says she's got nothing smaller than a twenty-pound note.

DAD   And all I've got – *He digs in his pocket* – is twelve pence.

WILL   *exasperated* Da-ad!

MUFFY   Poor Will.

WILL   At least somebody cares about me. Thank you, Muffy.

Dad glances at the clock.

DAD   Your mother's going to be late. Here, take this tray up to her, will you?

*Still clutching the book, **Will** clumsily tries to take hold of the tray.*

DAD   Can't you put that book down for a single moment?

WILL   I'm reading it.

DAD   For about the ninetieth time.

WILL   *sullenly* Seventh.

DAD   Careful! Don't slop the tea!

*Will takes the tray and turns, colliding with **Estelle** as she enters. Her hair is a rat's nest, her dressing gown is irregularly buttoned, and she has only one slipper on.*

DAD   Estelle! It's after eight already. Why aren't you dressed for school?

*Estelle lifts **Mum's** cup off the tray as she passes. **Dad** snatches it from her lips and puts it back on the tray, which **Will** carries out of the room.*

ESTELLE   Because I'm not going. I told you yesterday.

DAD   Don't think you did, dear.

ESTELLE   You never listen to anything I say.

DAD   I think I do. And anyway, you have to go to school, Estelle. It's the law.

ESTELLE   Then the law's stupid, isn't it?

DAD   And so will you be, dear, if you don't go.

*Estelle slumps at the table, snatches **Muffy's** milk, and picks up a pop magazine.*

DAD   *firmly*   Coffee, before you go back upstairs to get dressed, Estelle?

ESTELLE   No.

DAD   No, **what**?

ESTELLE   *with real venom*   No, **thank** you!

DAD   *brightly*   That's better, dear. Now tell me what's bothering you.   *He turns to open a cupboard door and adds into it, under his breath*   You miserable, bad-tempered old maggot.

Estelle raises her head sharply.

ESTELLE   What did you say?

DAD   I said, 'Tell Daddy why you don't feel like going to school today'.

ESTELLE   It's not just that I 'don't feel like it'. I'm not going. It's just a waste of time. I've gone for years and years, and I'm not going any longer. I've had enough.

DAD   You have to go to school, Estelle. It's education, you see. Education. It's what distinguishes . . .   *Proudly, he throws out his chest*   Man . . .   *He snatches her pop magazine and opens it at the centrefold of an unsavoury rock star*   . . . from Animal.

Estelle snatches back the magazine.

ESTELLE   Not in our school, it isn't. We never get to learn anything. We never do anything interesting. And, if we do, Mark Hanley and Rick Sheens muck about all the time and ruin it. So I'm not going. It's just a waste of time.

*Mum comes in, wearing a smart suit and riffling through the papers in her briefcase. **Will** is trailing after her.*

WILL   You must have some money somewhere.

MUM   Will, do stop trailing after me and whingeing. What's just a waste of time, Estelle?

ESTELLE   Going to school.

MUM   It can't all be a waste of time, Estelle. You must have learned something over the years. You can **read**, can't you?

3

Mum *turns to the mirror and starts to adjust her hair.*

ESTELLE   You always claimed that it was you who taught me to read! You said if Miss Philomena had had her way, I'd still be staring at the pretty pictures!

MUM   Well, you can **write**.

ESTELLE   *outraged*   I like that! You're always on at me about my writing!

DAD   Well, you **know** things. You know where places like France and Russia are.

MUM   No, she doesn't.

ESTELLE   See? See? It's useless. You two have been going on for years and years about how useless it is.   *She makes the green fingernails of one hand chatter to their opposite numbers, imitating her parents*   'What does she **do** all day, that's what I'd like to know?' 'Well, she certainly doesn't seem to learn much!' 'I don't think they even bother to look at her work.' 'They most certainly don't bother to correct it.'

Mum *and* ***Dad*** *exchange embarrassed glances.*

ESTELLE   *triumphantly*   **See?**

WILL   Dad, about my lunch money –

Dad *brushes* ***Will*** *aside.*

DAD   Naturally, Estelle, your mother and I share the occasional worry about how –

WILL   Da-ad!

ESTELLE   No, Dad! You can't have it both ways!   *She storms towards the door*   Ever since I first started at that school, you two have been going on about what a waste of time it is, and how little I learn. Now I'm agreeing with you. And you still want to shovel me out there. How hypocritical!

Estelle *leaves, banging the door. The room shakes.*

WILL   Mum, if I take the twenty pounds –

MUM   *to* ***Dad***   Estelle's certainly not staying home all day by herself.

DAD   Certainly not.

WILL   About my lunch money –

MUM   Will! Do stop following me around the room! It drives me mad!

Will almost explodes, then visibly controls himself.

MUFFY Poor Will!

WILL   Thank you, Muffy.

*With heavy tread, **Will** opens the fridge and stares morosely inside. There is nothing in it. He closes it again.*

MUM   Go up and tell her, George.

DAD   Tell her what?

MUM   Tell her she has to go to school, of course.

Will opens a cupboard and stares. Nothing. He closes it.

DAD   You tell her, Heather. You're her mother.

MUM   No, you tell her, George. You're her father.

Will opens another cupboard. Nothing.

DAD   For God's sake, Will. Stop opening and shutting all the cupboard doors. You're driving everyone **crazy**.

WILL   *outraged*   **I'm** driving everyone crazy? What about **me**? What about **my** problem? What about the fact that –

MUM   Will, do stop arguing.   *A face looms at the window* Look, Chopper's here. Why don't you two watch Muffy in the garden until it's time for her car pool?

WILL   *Holding out his hand*   Come on, Muff.

*Muffy slips off her chair. **Will** picks up his school bag and the book.*

DAD   *to Muffy*   Bye-bye, precious!

MUM   *to Muffy*   Ta-ra, sweet!

WILL   What about –

MUM
DAD } Will! Hurry up!

*Will and **Muffy** leave, hand in hand. **Mum** turns to **Dad**. Unnoticed, Chopper opens the window to eavesdrop.*

DAD   Now, are you going to tell her?

MUM   I think it should be you. She doesn't listen to a word I say.

DAD   She doesn't listen to a word I say, either!

Mum looks at the clock.

MUM   Oh, God!

DAD   Right! Let's charge together then!   *He pulls an imaginary soldier's cap straight on his head, pulls an imaginary pistol from an imaginary holster, and turns his wife to face the door, standing close behind her*   Safety in numbers. I'll give you covering fire. Ready?

Mum and Dad march together towards the door, brandishing their imaginary weaponry.

MUM   Over the top!

DAD   *firing*   Pkeu! Pkeu! Pkeu! Pkeu!

In the window, Chopper is shaking his head in utter disbelief.

SCENE TWO

In the garden. As Chopper turns from the window, Will and Muffy appear, hand in hand. Each holds a book in their free hand. Behind them is an empty rabbit pen and a closed hutch.

CHOPPER   Ready to go?

WILL   Just got to wait for Muffy's lift to come.

CHOPPER   Morning, Muff. What're you reading today? *He prises the book from Muffy's hand*   'Rumpelstiltskin' again, eh? Still on the same old book.   *He turns to Will and inspects his book, too*   Runs in the family, doesn't it? No change here, either. Still 'The Longest Summer'.

WILL   *defensively*   It's very interesting.

CHOPPER   It's not like you, though, is it? Will Fairway, Bookworm Extraordinaire. And here you are, reading the same old book for six whole weeks. He must spin a good yarn, this –   *He inspects the spine*   William Scott Saffery.   *He hands back the book*   Same first name as you.

WILL   Same age, too.

CHOPPER   *accusingly*   You said it was a war book. First world war memoirs, you told me.

WILL   So it is.

CHOPPER   How can it be? If it's his story, and he's only our age?

WILL   He lied to the army about his date of birth.

CHOPPER   And got away with it? Just like that?

WILL   The soldiers were dying in their thousands by then. The army wasn't checking.

CHOPPER   But, no older than us! And to be in a real war! Why on earth did he do it?

WILL   He really wanted to go. Listen to this.   *He riffles through the book until he finds the place*   'I know I face the unknown – danger, hardship, wounds, maybe even my own death. But I can think only of heroics, of battles won, of this great war I've read so much about in every newspaper. What if I'd missed it, being born too late? No need to worry, for I am here now, proud and glad. This will be my greatest adventure.'

CHOPPER   And was it? Is that why you're reading it over and over again? Because it's the greatest adventure?

WILL   Oh, no. He wrote that when he was only a few days in, still on the back of the lorry, watching the road unfold behind him.   *He opens the book again*   'Like a grey ribbon', he says. But after a few more days –

Will breaks off, and looks anxious.

CHOPPER   *prompting*   Yes? After a few more days?

WILL   I don't want to talk about it, Chopper.

CHOPPER   But you can't stop reading about it, can you? Whatever it is he has to tell is so astonishing you read about it over and over. You can't stop. The way you've been going round with your nose stuck in that book, you probably know his days and nights better than your own.

WILL   I told you, Chopper. I don't want to talk about it.   *He turns away*   Come on, Muffy. Let's go and say hello to Thumper before your lift comes.

Muffy gives a sharp intake of breath and covers her face

with her hands. It is as if she's just remembered something horrible.

CHOPPER What's wrong with her?

WILL *Dropping to his knees in front of her, and prising her fingers from her face* Muffy? Muffy, what's wrong?

Muffy points to the hutch and starts to sob noisily.

CHOPPER Something to do with your rabbit? Has she remembered something? Was it a dream?

WILL Was it, Muff? Was it a bad dream?

Muffy shakes her head violently.

WILL Not a dream. What is it then, Muffy?

Muffy points to the hutch again, and whimpers.

WILL Come on, sweetheart. If you won't talk, how can I understand what you want? Make with the words.

Covering her eyes with one hand, Muffy points to the hutch with the other. Behind her back, Chopper makes the curly-wurly-cuckoo sign.

CHOPPER Honestly, Will! Your family! Seriously strange! Your parents pretending that they're soldiers going over the top to winkle your sister out of her shell hole. Muffy not speaking ever –

WILL She does speak sometimes. Don't you, Muff?

Muffy nods.

CHOPPER She's not speaking now, though, is she?

WILL Just shut up, Chopper. Give her a chance.

Silence, with Chopper looking I-told-you-so.

WILL Muffy, if you don't tell me what you're on about, how can I sort it out?

MUFFY *with an effort* Stelly!

WILL Did Estelle do something to Thumper?

Muffy shakes her mop of hair.

WILL Did she say something, then?

Muffy nods.

CHOPPER *impatiently* Do what your brother says,

8

Muffy. Make with the words or we'll be here all day. What did your sister say?

MUFFY *sticking out her bottom lip*   Said she was going to cook him!

WILL   Cook Thumper?

CHOPPER   Cook your rabbit? Ugh!

Muffy nods.

WILL   And now you're worried that he isn't in there, is that it? You can't see him, so you think she's gone and done it.

Muffy nods.

WILL   Oh, Muffy. You shouldn't let her wind you up.

CHOPPER   Why not? Everyone else lets her.

Will lifts the hutch top to reveal Thumper, perfectly content.

WILL   Happy now? Sure?

Muffy nods and picks up Thumper.

CHOPPER   She's turned into a positive **witch**, your sister.

WILL   She always **used** to be all right.

CHOPPER   *wistfully*   She used to be good fun. She used to let me run the bank in Monopoly, even though I get muddled.

WILL   She used to lend me her bike, even when she wanted it herself. Now, if I go near it, she flies out of her cage.

CHOPPER   She spat tintacks at me yesterday when I called her Stelly.

WILL   You never dared call her Stelly!

CHOPPER   We **used** to be able to call her Stelly.

WILL   She **used** to be all right.

A car hoot sounds. Muffy puts Thumper back in his hutch, and runs.

WILL   What have you forgotten, Muffy?

Muffy looks down at her book, confused.

WILL   No, not the book.

Muffy *runs back and hugs him. Then she's off again.*

CHOPPER What about me?

Muffy *panics. Then she runs back and hugs Chopper. The car hoot sounds again.* ***Muffy*** *flies off.*

WILL Bye!

CHOPPER She's sweet, your sister.

Estelle *steps out of the house, dressed unsuitably for school, plus a jacket. Nose in the air. Scowl on her face.*

CHOPPER Not like some people I could mention . . .

WILL Estelle! That's my jacket! You never even asked!

ESTELLE How should I know you two lame-brains were still hanging about?

CHOPPER Nice. Most polite. Very friendly.

ESTELLE Oh, stuff it, Chopper. Sarcasm doesn't suit you. Neither does that haircut.

CHOPPER Charming!

Will *steps back, imitating terror, flattening himself against the hedge. He holds up his fingers in the shape of a cross.*

WILL See that thing there, Chopper? It **looks** right, doesn't it? And it **sounds** right. It even **walks** right. But beware, Chopper! Beware! That thing there is NOT MY SISTER!

CHOPPER *in a gravelly, horror-film voice* 'Tis the dark creature who hath crawled from the fresh grave. Those who do hear her wail by day lie cold as stones by nightfall.

ESTELLE Oh, shut up, you great thimble-brain!

CHOPPER Cover your ears!

WILL And watch her floating by, pale wraith of death –

Estelle *adjusts the jacket around her shoulders.*

WILL – pulling her cloak around her bony shoulders like a shroud.

CHOPPER Banshee! Banshee!

WILL The Banshee of Beechcroft Avenue!

CHOPPER Banshee! Banshee!

Estelle *disappears through the gate.* ***Will*** *and* ***Chopper*** *fall* *about laughing. Then* **Will** *claps a hand to the back of his neck.*

WILL   Ouch!   *He swings round to look after* **Estelle**   She hit me!

Chopper *picks up the stone and inspects it.*

CHOPPER   Look at it. All nasty sharp bits. She's a fiend in human shape, that sister of yours.

WILL   Gran thinks it's demonic possession.

CHOPPER   I think it's war.

WILL   War?

CHOPPER   Yes, war. Your family's like a little platoon of soldiers huddled in their trench, waiting for the next attack. Muffy's got shell shock. That's why she hardly speaks. Your parents creep round in pairs, reconnoitring. Even your rabbit stays safely under cover.

WILL   I suppose you're right. It is a bit like that.

CHOPPER   I don't know why you bother reading William Saffery's war memoirs all the time. The life you're leading, you could write your own.

WILL   *ruefully*   I could, too!

CHOPPER   That's what I'm saying. You could.

Chopper *picks up his school bag.* **Will** *stands stock-still, thinking.*

CHOPPER   Are you coming?

WILL   I really could. I could do just what William Scott Saffery did. He was an impeccable war reporter. He turned himself into the very ears and eyes of war, and grimly wrote it all down, every last horror, exactly as it happened.

CHOPPER   *impatiently, from the gate*   Are you coming, Will?

WILL   Yes, I'm coming.   *He hastily shoves his copy of 'The Longest Summer' in the hutch*   And I won't need to carry you around with me any more. I'll write my own book. *He pulls an exercise book from his school bag*   In here. I'll keep a strict account of everything that happens. Every small skirmish. Every major battle. I'll note the casualties. I'll assess the damage.

CHOPPER *off* Will! I'm going without you now!

WILL Coming! *Triumphantly, **Will** spreads his arms*
The Impeccable War Reporter! That'll be me! *He runs
off, after **Chopper*** Wait for me!

ACT TWO

SCENE ONE

Early morning, a week later. **Mum** *and* **Dad***'s bedroom.*
Mum *is hidden beneath the duvet.* **Dad** *is sitting on the bed,
putting on his dressing gown and yawning. There is a tap on
the door.*

DAD   Yes? Come in. What is it?

Will *comes in. The exercise book is rolled up in his back
pocket.*

WILL   I was just wondering about my lunch money
   because –

Estelle *bursts in behind* **Will** *and pushes him aside.*

ESTELLE   I need five pounds.

The mound that is **Mum** *rises in the bed. Hastily,* **Dad**
pushes it down again. **Will** *whips the exercise book out of his
back pocket, settles on his heels against the wall, out of the
line of fire, and starts taking notes, eyeing each protagonist
and scribbling furiously.*

DAD   Excuse me, Estelle?

ESTELLE   *impatiently*   I need five pounds. For school.

DAD   Five pounds!

ESTELLE   Yes. This morning.

DAD   But what's it for?

ESTELLE   For a **field** trip. To Sanderley **Tree** Park.
   I **told** you.

DAD   Not sure you did, Estelle.

ESTELLE   It's not **my** fault if you don't listen to me.

13

The hump in the bed rises again. **Dad** *pushes it down again.*

DAD   We do listen to you, Estelle. It's just that neither your mother nor I remembers hearing you say anything at all about needing five pounds for a field trip.

ESTELLE   I suppose you think I'm lying!

DAD   That's not very nice, Estelle. And it's not fair, either. I don't believe you're lying. I'd just like you to have the good manners to tell me a little bit about this field trip before I dip in my wallet to pay for it.

ESTELLE   You hate spending money on anything to do with me, don't you?

DAD   Don't be ridiculous, Estelle!

ESTELLE   I'm not. You buy things for the others happily enough. You bought Muffy a whole bed last week.

The mound behind **Dad** *rises again. This time, he has to throw his whole weight on it to force it down again.*

DAD   Estelle, Muffy can't sleep in a cot bed forever!

ESTELLE   And you bought Will that calculator!

Will stops scribbling in his exercise book. His mouth drops open and he stares at his sister.

DAD   He's taking **Maths**, Estelle.

ESTELLE   And all I ask you for is five miserable pounds to go with the rest of my class to Sanderley Tree Park, and you end up giving me a giant great row!

Estelle slams out. The mound beside **Dad** *is making odd, incoherent-with-wrath noises. Slowly, he lets it rise.* **Mum** *appears, breathing deeply to try to regain her temper.* **Will** *scribbles the last words, muttering under his breath.*

WILL   '. . . end up giving me a giant great row.' There!

Satisfied, **Will** *rolls up the exercise book and puts it back in his pocket. He turns to* **Dad***, who is patting* **Mum** *to soothe her.*

WILL   About my lunch money . . .

DAD   Oh, Will. Do stop going on about money all the time. Don't you think your mother's got enough to cope with, with your sister flying off the handle every few minutes?

Will steps experimentally on the scales in the corner.

WILL   I'm losing weight, you know.

Muffy pushes open the door and comes in.

WILL   Yesterday I had a crust for lunch. Literally, a crust! The day before, I had a shrivelled carrot and four of Muffy's liquorice allsorts. The day before that, I had to have salad cream on crackers.

MUFFY   *tragically, with a huge effort*   Poor Will!

WILL   See? Even Muffy's speaking up for me. She knows. I am a growing lad, and I need proper food.

MUM   *laughing*   Oh, Will! You win. Just let me get dressed, and then I'll look in my purse. You'll have your lunch today.

Estelle storms back in, pushing *Will* aside as before.

ESTELLE   Oh, I forgot to tell you. Alison's having a party tonight, and I'm going. That's all right, isn't it?

Estelle turns to go. *Will* whips out his notebook again. *Dad* steps in front of *Estelle* to prevent her leaving.

DAD   Alison? Alison who?

ESTELLE   You know!

DAD   *suspiciously*   Refresh my memory.

ESTELLE   You met her!

MUM   Was she that nice girl we met once at the swimming pool?

Estelle looks shifty.

DAD   No. Wasn't she that one Estelle disappeared with in the arcade? The one you said looked like something that just crawled out of a gr–   *Hastily, **Dad** corrects himself* –the one whose clothes you noticed.

MUM   *horrified*   Not her! It's not that Alison, is it, Estelle?

ESTELLE   What does it matter which Alison it is? She's my friend, not yours! And I'm the one who's going to her party.

DAD   Will her parents be there?

MUM   And what time will it finish?

ESTELLE   How should I know what time it's going to finish? It hasn't even started yet!

DAD   No need to get fresh, young lady!

MUM   Estelle, if you can't tell us what time this party's going to finish, how can we arrange to pick you up?

ESTELLE   You're not picking me up! I'm not a baby like Muffy!

Muffy looks crushed. Will looks up from note-taking.

WILL   Ignore her, Muffy. She's just being rude.

MUM   It isn't **babyish** to be picked up, Estelle. It's **sensible**.

ESTELLE   I'll be all right. I'll **walk** home.

Estelle turns to the mirror, picks something off the dresser and starts to fiddle with some eyeliner around her eyes.

MUM   Not late at night you won't, Estelle!

DAD   We haven't even agreed she can go yet!

ESTELLE   Everyone else is going! Why can't **I**?

Will is clearly losing track with his notes because of the speed and ferocity of the argument.

WILL   *muttering*   '. . . **walk** home'.

DAD   Nobody's said you **can't**. We just haven't said you **can** yet.

ESTELLE   You're always trying to spoil things for me!

MUM   What about you, Estelle? Doesn't it ever occur to you that you're spoiling things for other people? What about Muffy? You've just spoiled her morning by calling her a baby.

WILL   And what about m–?

MUM   *interrupting*   And what about Will? The poor boy never manages to get a word in edgeways with you going on all the time. Why can't you show a bit of self-control? Why can't we just get through **one single morning** without –

Estelle turns round. She looks like a raccoon.

MUM   Estelle! That eye stuff costs twenty pounds a refill!

DAD   Wipe that stuff off your face at once! You look like a dockside tart!

WILL *muttering desperately* '. . . dockside tart'.

ESTELLE Well, can I go, or can't I?

DAD Don't take that tone with me!

MUM Yes, watch your tongue, Estelle!

ESTELLE I don't see why I have to go round never saying what I think, and not sticking up for myself, just so Muffy and Will can grow up in some sort of fairy tale.

DAD There's nothing fairy-tale about preferring not to have a fight five seconds after waking up.

MUM Yes. Well done, Estelle. Another morning ruined.

ESTELLE Oh, that's right! Blame me! Of course it has to be **my** fault! All right, then. I'll go to school now, and I'll go without my five pounds. And when Miss Sullivan asks me why I'm the only one in my whole year who hasn't gone on the field trip to Sanderley Tree Park, I'll tell her it's because you wouldn't pay for it!

*Estelle leaves, slamming the door. **Will** flinches, but keeps scribbling. **Mum** is speechless with fury. **Dad** roots fruitlessly in his own pockets, then dives for **Mum's** purse.*

WILL *looking up* No, Dad! No!

*But it's too late – **Dad** flings all the money out of the window at the departing **Estelle**.*

DAD There! Take your money! Go on your bloody field trip! Don't let us stop you! Go out in the country and have a nice day kicking blackbirds and spitting at the rabbits!

Muffy claps her hands over her ears in horror.

MUFFY *wailing* Ooooh!

Will scribbles furiously for a few more seconds.

WILL *muttering* '. . . spitting at the rabbits.'

*Will stops. There is absolute silence. **Dad** is leaning, exhausted, out of the window. **Mum** has her head in her hands. **Muffy** is frozen, as if a shell is about to fall on her. The silence lasts.*

WILL William Scott Saffery says there is no silence like the silence after an attack. It has, he says, a quality so real you can reach out and touch it.

DAD   *mystified*   William Scott **who**? Said **what**?

WILL   Nothing.

MUM   Oh, God! Look at the time! Another late morning. I'm going to lose my job.

*Desperately, **Mum** gathers up her things to rush to the bathroom. **Dad** is rushing to get ready, too.*

DAD   Muffy! Quick! Go and get ready for school!

***Muffy** rushes out of the room.*

WILL   About my lunch money.

MUM   Oh, Will! I haven't got time to think about that now. ***Mum** rushes out.*

WILL   Dad?

DAD   For God's sake, lad! Can't you see there's a war on? ***Dad** rushes out after **Mum**.*

WILL   *to the audience*   Oh, I can see there's a war on. I've only been at it a week, and my exercise book is half-filled up already.   *He taps the exercise book*   I reckon William Scott Saffery wouldn't scoff at some of the battles in here. I even caught Mum hitching up her skirt and climbing in through the back window yesterday, so she didn't have to go through the kitchen and past Estelle.   *He looks down to read from his notes*   'All I need is five minutes', she said when she saw me watching her. 'Five minutes of peace and quiet. Then I can face it. I'll just have one little gin and tonic.' So I told her: 'They gave them rum in the trenches'. 'Trenches!' she scoffed. And you could tell she'd happily sell our whole house (with Estelle in it) to get a nice, quiet trench on the front line.

***Mum** comes back from the bathroom.*

MUM   Trenches? Are you talking to yourself about trenches? I tell you, Will, those war memoirs you keep reading have finally turned your brain. You're going mad.

***Will** rolls up his exercise book and hides it in his back pocket. **Mum** scuttles round, finishing dressing.*

MUM   Now go and do something useful. Since your Dad seems to have flung all my money at Estelle, you'd better make yourself a sandwich for school.

WILL   There's nothing in the fridge.

MUM   How come?

WILL   You said that you were going to do the shopping yesterday, but then the whole evening got used up with that argument with Estelle.

MUM   Which argument with Estelle?

*Turning his back, **Will** surreptitiously whips out his exercise book and flicks through.*

WILL   The argument about whether she could go out wearing that purple spotted skirt. You said, 'You can't go out in that! It shows your –'

MUM   *hastily*   Oh, **that** argument. Well, never mind. I promise your Dad and I will get the shopping done tonight. I promise this won't happen again. You'll have your lunch tomorrow. Honestly, Will.

***Dad** rushes in, putting on his tie.*

DAD   What's the problem now?

MUM   There's no more food again.

DAD   No food?   *He shrugs*   Well, that's war for you, Will.

WILL   *irritated*   It's not **my** war, though, is it?

DAD   No picnickers in wartime, Will, my boy. You can't know anything if you don't know that. 'He who is not with me is against me.' Everyone has to take a side in war. Come on now, Heather. Hurry up.

***Mum** and **Dad** gather their things, and leave the bedroom.*

WILL   And how am I supposed to take a side? I don't know which side I'm on. William Scott Saffery didn't have this problem. They handed him a uniform, and it was khaki, and he put it on. They handed him a rifle, and he was supposed to point it at anybody wearing field grey. But it's not like that in a family. Sometimes I'd come down on Estelle's side. Sometimes on theirs.

***Dad** pokes his head around the door.*

DAD   Will, are you going to hang around daydreaming all day? Or are you going to school? Chopper's waiting!

Dad disappears.

WILL   At least that's one thing I know. Chopper's a mate. And he's always on my side. No problems there!

Will leaves the room.

SCENE TWO

Chopper and Will are on the street on the way to school.

CHOPPER   I reckon you are totally, one hundred per cent in the wrong!

WILL   Well, thanks, mate! Thanks a bunch!

CHOPPER   No, seriously, Will. I'll prove it.   *He draws out a coin*   Toss for a colour. Brown or grey?

WILL   *shrugging*   Brown.

CHOPPER   OK. So, heads or tails?

WILL   Tails.

Chopper tosses the coin and inspects it.

CHOPPER   You win. So you're brown.

WILL   Brown what?

CHOPPER   Brown uniform, of course. Khaki. And I'm field grey.

Chopper steps back behind the cover of a hedge, and fires at Will without warning with an imaginary sub-machine-gun.

CHOPPER   TA-TA-TA-TA-TA-TA-TA-TA-TA-TA-TA-TA-TA!

Chopper raises his head over the hedge.

CHOPPER   Go on, then! Defend yourself! I'm shooting at you!

Will drops back behind a lamppost, and fires back.

WILL   TA-TA-TA-TA-TA-TA! TA-TA-TA-TA-TA!

Estelle, engrossed in a book, comes round the corner.

WILL   Get down, Estelle! You'll get shot!

ESTELLE   What are you two dim-bulbs up to now?

WILL   Estelle! Be careful! You'll get killed!

*Will steps out and drags **Estelle** behind the lamppost with him. She wallops him. He drops his imaginary weapon. **Chopper** seizes the chance to step out and aim at point-blank range.*

CHOPPER   Ah-ha!

WILL   Not so fast, buster!

Will snatches up his weapon and fires first.

WILL   TA-TA-TA-TA! Gotcha! You're dead!

CHOPPER   *cooperatively*   If you say so . . .

*Chopper steps out, staggers spectacularly, then takes his time dying dramatically. **Will** prods the corpse with his toe. **Chopper** gets up and brushes himself down fastidiously.*

WILL   So what did all that prove?

CHOPPER   That you're totally and one hundred per cent in the wrong. It **is** as stupid as that. Either a soldier happens to be born here –   *He points to one side*   – and fetches up fighting on this side. Or he's born there –   *He points to the other side*   – and ends up fighting back. Then either they live, or they get shot. The whole thing's just a matter of accident. It's the stupidest way of settling arguments that anyone ever invented.

WILL   So everyone who ever fought in any war was just a half-wit? Is that it?

CHOPPER   Just about, yes.

WILL   *sarcastically*   Every last million of them. All idiots, right?

CHOPPER   Not far off.

WILL   So what would someone **intelligent** – say like that handsome, clever, educated lad, R. M. Chopperly –

*With a great flourish, **Chopper** takes a bow.*

CHOPPER   The very same!

WILL   What would he do, if, God forbid, he was called up for some daft war he couldn't see the point of fighting properly?

CHOPPER   I hope I'd have the sense to run away. Failing that, hope for the best: flat feet; rotten eyesight –

Estelle looks up from her book.

21

ESTELLE   Not like the mad keen lemmings in this book.

CHOPPER   What book?

ESTELLE   This one. I found it in the rabbit hutch. It's all about someone your age who fetches up in some war he ends up thinking is a waste of time, and he just keeps on fighting.

WILL   Estelle! That's my book!

ESTELLE   *coolly*   I don't think so, Will. I just borrowed it from Thumper.

WILL   You can't keep it!

ESTELLE   Don't worry. I shan't want to. It's stuffed full with idiots like those ancient aunts of ours.

CHOPPER   Which ancient aunts? Those two old frost-tops who showed up last Christmas?

WILL   No, these were even older than that. In fact, they're so old, they're dead now. Gran told us all about them the day Estelle was nosing through her box of souvenirs, and found some ancient photos.

ESTELLE   I was not 'nosing'. I was taking an interest.

WILL   Anyhow, she found these really old photos. Two of them.

ESTELLE   Almost **exactly** the same.

WILL   Of Gran's aunties, sitting in a row on a bench at the seaside.

ESTELLE   Rose, Elsie, Greta –

WILL   Matty and Daisy.

ESTELLE   All dressed exactly the same, in fancy long dresses with matching parasols. Except that, in one of the photos, they were all in white –

WILL   And in the other, they were all in black. And Gran explained. The photo where they were all wearing white was taken in the summer at the start of the Great War.

ESTELLE   In 1914.

WILL   When the aunts were all young and courting, or only just married.

ESTELLE   And the other was taken four years later.

WILL   In 1918.

CHOPPER   *thoughtfully*   And they were all dressed in

black. So someone got killed.

ESTELLE   Not someone. Everyone. Gran ticked them off, and there were so many that she ran out of fingers halfway through. Fathers, husbands, brothers, uncles, fiancés, friends . . . And the aunts were just sitting there, on the same bench.

WILL   And the worst of it, Gran said, was that, all through those summers on the beach, watching the children, they could hear, far away across the Channel, the endless pounding of the guns in France, killing and wounding everyone they cared about.

ESTELLE   And they just sat there. Like sheep. Except that sheep would probably have shown a lot more spirit and a lot more sense.

WILL   Stelly!

ESTELLE   Don't 'Stelly' me! It's no more than the truth.

WILL   Gran said that every time a black-edged telegram came to the house –

ESTELLE   *interrupting*   I know! 'They were destroyed!' But, of course, they were better brought up than to show it! Oh, no! Stiff upper lip! No fussing. No asking troublesome questions, like: 'What's it all **for**?' and 'How much waste can people **stand**?' No. Our dear ancient aunts just sat there bravely in a row, dressed all in black, and had their photo taken, just as usual.

CHOPPER   Horrible!

ESTELLE   It's worse than horrible! It's criminal and stupid! And I think that, like your precious William Scott Saffery in this book, every last one of them was just a fool and a coward.

WILL   Oh, not a coward! No!

ESTELLE   He was, Will. Really, he was! He says in here he knew after only a few weeks just what a shambles and a waste it all was. *She stabs a page*   Listen to this! 'I flung myself back in the ditch and all I could think about was what I'd say if, just for one hour, I was given the chance to show the "Big Brass" round the battlefield. Oh, I'd have horrors enough to show them! And I would let them know just what I thought of their great "war to end wars"!' Hear the anger in that, Will? Hear the sarcasm?

So why is it **himself** he's throwing in the ditch? Why isn't it his **rifle**?

WILL   You can't do that in war.

ESTELLE   You can.

WILL   Nobody does, though, Estelle.

ESTELLE   I would.

CHOPPER   *half admiringly*   I bet she would, too, Will.

WILL   And then your commanding officer would put a gun to your head.

ESTELLE   She'd have to fire it, too!

WILL   Maybe she would!

ESTELLE   And maybe, if there were enough behind me with guts enough to stand up to her as well, she wouldn't dare. She'd realise that, killing all of us, she'd lose her army even quicker than all those generals in the First World War managed to lose theirs!

WILL   They'd hush it up.

ESTELLE   You can't hush up scores and scores of black-edged telegrams. And maybe if all the good little people back at home were making a bit more of a fuss –

CHOPPER   Is that your bus leaving, Estelle? That one that says Sanderley Tree Park on the front?

ESTELLE   I'm not bothering. Tree parks are stupid.

WILL   If you're not going, you can hand over some of that five pounds so I can buy some lunch.

CHOPPER   Who is that waving at you from the back seat? Is it Flora? I can see that's Marisa at the front, trying to get the driver to stop.

ESTELLE   Is she? Oh, maybe I will go. If they're trying to stop the bus.

*Estelle tosses the book to **Will**, and runs off.*

ESTELLE   Bye! Stop that bus! Stop it at once! Wait for me! Can't you see I'm coming? STOP!

There is a screech of brakes.

WILL   Well, thanks a bunch, Chopper! You've spiked my last chance of a decent lunch.

CHOPPER   Sorry. I thought you'd like a few precious hours of cease-fire.

WILL   So I would. If I wasn't too hungry to enjoy them.

CHOPPER   You can share the lunch I've got.

WILL   What's that, then?

Chopper peers in his bag.

CHOPPER   Two bacon, lettuce and tomato sandwiches. Banana. Apple. A huge lump of cheese.

WILL   Banquet!

CHOPPER   Four chocolate biscuits. A carton of strawberry milk. And a yoghurt. Unless it's curdled from that sister of yours walking right past it . . .

WILL   Probably has. Forget the yoghurt.

Chopper stares in the direction of the bus.

CHOPPER   Boy, is she fierce! I sure as hell wouldn't want Estelle on **my** side in any war!

*Will looks a bit confused. Then, with a rumble of engines, the bus goes past. Automatically, **Chopper** and **Will** raise their fingers in the protective shape of the cross.*

CHOPPER   Banshee! Banshee!

WILL   Banshee!

*It is clear that, on the back seat, **Estelle**, **Flora** and **Marisa** are waggling their hands insultingly against their ears, and sticking out their tongues, until the bus is out of sight.*

CHOPPER   That's it, then.   *He inspects his watch*   I make that seven hours of safety.

Will spins around, arms outstretched.

WILL   Cease-fire! Cease-fire! No sudden attacks! No shells spinning out of nowhere, blasting me apart. No grinding barrage of fire! Just seven hours of perfect, precious safety!   *Spilling possessions around him, he throws himself on his back, arms flung wide, like an exhausted soldier*   Apart from school, peace, perfect peace!

Chopper picks up a stray paper bag.

CHOPPER   What's this in here?

WILL   *lifting his head for a moment*   That? That's my lunch.

Chopper lifts out the saddest, most shrivelled sandwich on earth.

CHOPPER   But what **is** it?

WILL   It's Oxo cube sprinkled on Thumper's leftovers.

*Wrinkling his nose in disgust, **Chopper** peels it apart and inspects it. Then he looks thoughtfully at **Will**, still happily spreadeagled on the floor.*

CHOPPER   You're cracking up, Will Fairway. In fact, if you want my opinion, your entire family is now cracking up.

WILL   That's war for you, Private Chopperly.   *He stretches luxuriously*   And war is **hell**.

*Nearby, a school bell rings loudly. **Will** scrambles to his feet, and he and **Chopper** run off.*

SCENE THREE

*That evening. In the kitchen. **Muffy** and **Will** sit together. **Muffy** is pushing the book 'Rumpelstiltskin' towards her brother, and he is pushing it back.*

WILL   No, not again. I'm sick of it. I must have read it to you twenty million times. Anyway, I'm hungry.   *He trawls through the cupboards*   We're out of soup, of course. How about toast? Oh, no. I forgot. And there's no fruit. Somebody's even eaten that dead celery. We're going to have to starve till they get back.

Muffy pushes the book at him again.

WILL   Oh, all right. Nothing else to do after all. 'Once upon a time, in a faraway country, there lived –'

*There is a clatter at the back door as **Mum** and **Dad** come in.*

MUM   Stop trampling on my heels, George. I'm going as fast as I can.

DAD   I'm sorry. I couldn't see where I was going, what with you banging the door in my face.

MUM   Don't snap at me because the hinges don't work properly.

Mum dumps her briefcase on the table.

DAD   I'm sorry, Heather. It's been a difficult day. Two of the mechanics are off sick, and I had to man the phones and do a couple of servicings, as well as keeping my eye on that new girl on the forecourt.

MUM   Well, my day wasn't a picnic either, George. I had clients all morning, and a meeting all afternoon. And in my lunch break I had to go to the bank, pay the road tax, and pick up the tickets for that puppet show for Muffy.

Dad plugs in the kettle.

DAD   We'll both feel better after a cup of tea.

Will upends the canister to show that it's empty.

MUM   Oh, for heaven's sake! Can you make coffee then, Will? At least that'll perk me up.

WILL   There's only that herbal coffee of Aunt Lucy's left.

DAD   What's going on in here? *He trawls the cupboards in exactly the same order as Will* No bread. Out of muffins. No more tea. There's nothing in these cupboards.

MUM   That's because nobody's shopped for over a week. Nobody's had the time.

DAD   Will, nip down to the corner shop and get –

MUM   No, George! We're out of everything. We need to do a proper shop. Take the car. Stack up on everything.

DAD   I'm not going out again tonight! I'm absolutely **exhausted**.

MUM   You can't be more tired than I am. I can barely **stand**.

Mum sinks into a chair.

DAD   I warn you, Heather, I am incapable of leaving this house again this evening. Especially not to go shopping.

MUM   Somebody has to go, George. And I'm at the end of my rope. I cannot lift a finger. I am **destroyed**.

WILL *conversationally* Chopper says he thinks everybody in our family is falling apart.

DAD *icily* Oh, yes?

MUM Excuse me, but I don't think I quite see what business our household is of Rupert Chopperly's. Perhaps if that young man worried a little more about –

The door flies open.

ESTELLE *off* Aaaa-chooo!

Estelle comes in.

ESTELLE Aaachooo! Aaaachoooo! Aaachoo!

DAD Have a nice day, dear?

Estelle peels off her coat to reveal a jumper.

WILL Estelle! That's my best woolly! Take it off!

ESTELLE Aachoo!

Estelle peels the jumper off and drops it on the floor.

WILL Estelle!

ESTELLE It's sodden wet anyway. And covered in mud. And grass stains. And I caught the sleeve on a bramble, so some of it's come a bit undone.

Will lifts it up. It's a rag.

WILL Estelle! That was my birthday present from Gran!

ESTELLE Oh, lovely! Worry about your stupid jumper! Don't worry about me freezing to death on a boring old field trip!

MUM Will's quite within his rights to get annoyed, Estelle.

WILL She didn't even **ask**!

ESTELLE That's right! Start picking on me before I'm even through the door!

MUM Nobody's picking on you, Estelle. It's simply time you came to realise that –

Mum notices Dad tiptoeing towards the back door.

MUM George! Where are you going?

DAD Somebody has to do the shopping, dear. And I thought I would save you the trouble.

MUM Oh, no, George. No, no, no. I'll save **you** the trouble, honestly. You stay here and mind the children –

ESTELLE I'm not a child! I don't need looking after!

MUM *to Dad* You stay here and mind the house. And I'll nip out and get the shopping done.

Will gets out his exercise book and starts writing.

DAD No, no, no, Heather. You can't go back out again. You're absolutely exhausted. Don't forget you had clients all morning, a meeting all afternoon, and even in your lunchtime you had to go to the bank, pay the road tax, and pick up the tickets for Muffy's puppet show. You stay here and watch the chi-

ESTELLE *yelling* I'm not –

DAD House! And I'll go and do the shopping.

MUM No, no, George. Your day wasn't a picnic, either. What with your mechanics being off sick, and having to man the phones all by yourself. Not to mention doing the servicings and keeping your eye on that new girl on the forecourt. You stay and have a rest. Look after everyone. And I'll be back with the shopping in no time.

Mum snatches up her purse and makes for the door. Dad follows her closely, trying to pull her back.

DAD No, no. You stay. I'll go.

MUM No, really! I'll go. You stay.

Estelle puts her hand on her hips.

ESTELLE Oh, lovely! Very nice for me! I'm hardly back inside the door, and you two are squabbling about which one can get away!

Mum and Dad exchange hunted looks.

DAD I know! Let's both go!

MUM What a good idea! I'll need someone to help me carry.

DAD Of course you will!

MUM Look after Muffy, both of you. We won't be long.

There is a struggle as Mum and Dad both try to leave first. The door shuts behind them.

ESTELLE Charming! Very friendly, I must say! Very caring!

*Estelle turns. Hastily, **Will** hides his exercise book.*

ESTELLE   Well, I'm not wasting my time looking after Muff. You do it, Will.

Estelle makes for the door.

WILL   Excuse me. It's your turn.

ESTELLE   I'm busy, Will!

WILL   Yes, maybe you are. But it's still your turn to look after Muffy.

ESTELLE   Oh, do stop going on, Will!

WILL   I'm not going on. I'm simply telling you –

Estelle loses her temper, and stamps her foot.

ESTELLE   Shut up! Shut up! Shut up!

Muffy claps her hands over her ears and shuts her eyes.

WILL   Estelle, I've been looking after Muffy ever since we got back. I've read her 'Rumpelstiltskin' four times already –

ESTELLE   More fool you!

WILL   And now I need –

ESTELLE   You're talking to yourself, Will!

Estelle goes out and slams the door behind her.

WILL   I don't believe this! I might as well call this war report 'The Book of the Banshee'! She's such a **witch**! She is about the most selfish creature on this planet. She thinks of no one except herself. She is –

*Will catches sight of **Muffy** cowering miserably.*

WILL   Hey, Muff! Muffy!

Gently, he prises her hands away from her ears.

WILL   Open your eyes, Muffy. Look at me. Come on! She's gone now. Open your eyes. It's all safe.

*Tentatively, **Muffy** opens her eyes. **Will** pats the seat beside him.*

WILL   Come on. Sit down. Sit here.

*Muffy sits down. **Will** pats her knee.*

WILL   OK? Better?

Muffy *nods. They sit quietly for a moment.*

WILL Muffy, can you remember how things used to be?

Muffy *looks blank.*

WILL What I mean is, can you remember what things were like in this house before Estelle went all funny? Can you remember when we used to get up, live our lives peacefully, and then go to bed again? And there was none of this – none of this – **shambles**! This is like **war**, Muffy. This is what William Scott Saffery described when he crawled out of his trench once, and saw the hell's wilderness around him for what it was, and wondered what sort of force it was that could make so many millions of men vie with one another to make their world such a **mess**.

Muffy *pats* **Will** *comfortingly.*

MUFFY Poor Will. Poor Stelly.

WILL Poor Stelly! Oh, I don't know. Maybe you're right. Maybe she's not happy, either. She used to be such an angel. Do you remember? Even though I'm a whole year older, she used to be put in charge. They used to say to her, 'Be sure and hold Will's hand crossing the road'. And it was years before I realised they meant for her to look after me, and not the other way round. She was always the grown-up one.

Will *holds up his jumper, which looks like a muddy rag.*

MUFFY Poor woolly.

WILL I expect it's ruined. I don't understand. I always thought that people grew up bit by bit, learning one thing at a time. How can you start growing backwards? How can you **know** you have to ask before you take other people's stuff, and then forget again, and start to act as if you don't even understand how they're going to feel when they find their jumper, or their jacket, or the tapes they saved up to buy, all over the floor?

Muffy *shrugs.*

WILL Everyone's got their own way of describing what's happened.

Will *flicks through the exercise book and picks out examples.*

WILL   See here. Dad says that Estelle's 'gone a bit awkward'. Here, Mum says she's 'curdled'. Gran says *imitating* 'She gets a bit difficult at times'. And you? All through this notebook you just plaster your hands over your ears and shut your eyes tight.

Muffy looks embarrassed.

WILL   Oh, yes. And you stopped talking, of course. Except to say 'Poor Will' and 'Poor Stelly'. You know your problem, Muff? You're too like me. You haven't got it in you to fight back. You just hide in your books.   *Will reaches for 'Rumpelstiltskin'*   Anyway, where were we? *He reads*   'And then the bad-tempered little creature stamped his foot hard, and ran off into the black night . . .' *He glances towards the door through which* **Estelle** *left*   No wonder you like this so much, Muff.   *He starts to read again*   'And then the miller's daughter went down the stone stairs, into the great hall. And the prince took her hand . . .'

The lights fade as **Will's** *voice fades away.*

SCENE FOUR

An hour later. In the kitchen. The lights brighten and **Will's** *voice gradually gets louder as he reads to* **Muffy***.*

WILL   '. . . and, when the prince peeped into the cradle, he saw that the miller's daughter had given him the perfect child.'

Mum and Dad stagger in with the groceries.

MUM   The perfect child!

DAD   No such thing!

MUM   Wish we had one!

WILL   What's wrong with me and Muffy, then?

Mum and Dad dump their groceries on the table and start to unpack.

MUM   Tell him, George.

DAD   No, you tell him, Heather.

WILL   See? You can't think of anything.

MUM   Can't think of anything? Do you really think you're that easy to live with? Blaring that frightful music out of your room night and day?

DAD   Disappearing into your bedroom at the first sign of having to pitch in with the housework.

MUM   Sticking those horrible posters all over your nice honeysuckle wallpaper.

DAD   Shambling around the house like something Frankenstein knocked up at night.

MUM   Picking the leaves off the houseplants and eating them.

DAD   Bursting through doors without stopping to turn the handle.

MUM   Chewing your bus tickets so half the time you end up having to pay twice.

DAD   Getting into all those stupid fights with Stormer Philips.

MUM   And setting fire to next door's shed like that.

WILL   That was an accident!

DAD   Pretty expensive accident!

WILL   Well, all right. I'll grant you I'm not perfect. You could have done a whole lot worse, though.

MUM   That's right. We could have had Chopper.

DAD   What's Chopper done now?

MUM   His Dad was just telling me over the frozen beans. Last night he stripped his bike down on a brand new carpet.

DAD   Stripped down his **bike**? On a **carpet**?

MUM   **Pools** of oil, Mr Chopperly told me. All trodden in, and splashed up all the walls. And great big black footprints all over.

WILL   It was a **speck**, Chopper said! You practically had to have a microscope to see it!

MUM   Not what his father just told me.

WILL   He was exaggerating, I expect. Just like you did that time you were telling him about Estelle dyeing her hair.

MUM   I did not exaggerate, Will. I simply told Mr and Mrs Chopperly exactly what Estelle ruined that day.

Estelle, in a dressing gown, opens the door, unnoticed by Mum, who is ticking the damaged items off on her fingers.

MUM   Namely: two snow-white bedspreads; three lengths of wallpaper; one little blue furry rug; her sweater; two towels; a flannel; and two library books.

Estelle rolls her eyes to heaven and shuts the door again.

WILL   Those library books weren't ruined. You could still read them.

MUM   **Not** what the library said. George, were there more boxes?

DAD   I'll bring them in. You put the car in the garage.

MUM   OK.

Mum and Dad go out of the back door. Estelle pokes her head round the inner door again.

ESTELLE   Why are they on about that time I dyed my hair?

WILL   They're not. You were only a sideline. They were really on about me.

Estelle comes in, buttoned up to the neck, and carrying a basket of make-up.

ESTELLE   I don't know why they bothered to have children. All they do is moan.

With Muffy watching, fascinated, Estelle starts to make up her face.

WILL   Why are you in your dressing gown?

ESTELLE   *smirking*   Wouldn't you like to know?

Muffy starts making up as well: green spots, silver lips, aubergine eyes.

WILL   You're wearing something underneath that, aren't you? What have you got on underneath?

ESTELLE   *singing provocatively*   La-la-la-la-la. La-la-la-la-la!

Like a stripper, Estelle unbuttons the dressing gown, and

*flashes. **Muffy** claps her hands in excitement. From top to toe,
Estelle is dressed in sexy, glittery and outrageous party gear.*

MUFFY *thrilled* Stelly!

WILL You still think you're going to Alison's party!

ESTELLE I don't just **think**. I **am**.

WILL They'll never let you. You don't stand a chance.
Especially not tarted up like that.

ESTELLE Mind your own business, will you?

WILL I'm only warning you.

ESTELLE Well, don't. Keep your nose out of this.

WILL I expect there are tigers better-tempered than you
are!

ESTELLE Just shut up, Will!

***Muffy's** smile has faded. She is creeping away to her book.*

WILL But you'll have to ask them. You can't just sneak
out.

ESTELLE I'll **tell** them.

WILL Good. Because here they come.

*Nervously, **Muffy** swings round. **Estelle**, though, has turned
away hastily to button up her dressing gown. So **Mum** and
Dad catch sight of **Muffy** first.*

MUM My God!

WILL It's all right. There's nothing wrong with her. She's
just been rooting about in Estelle's make-up basket.

DAD *suspiciously* In Estelle's make-up basket, eh?

***Dad** turns **Estelle** round so he can inspect her make-up.*

DAD My God!

WILL It's all right. There's nothing wrong with her, either.
She's just going out.

DAD Not looking like that, she isn't! And that's final!

***Dad** turns his back to help **Mum** with the unpacking.
Estelle sticks her tongue out at his back. **Muffy** holds her
hands ready, over her ears.*

MUM *in a conciliatory tone* Where were you thinking of
going, Estelle? Were you nipping down to the library
before it closes?

Estelle rolls her eyes contemptuously.

DAD   Perhaps she was thinking of helping Mrs Hurley with the Brownies.

Estelle's eyes roll again.

WILL   She says she's going to Alison's party.

ESTELLE   You're a pig, Will! A nosy, meddling pig!

Muffy claps her hands over her ears.

WILL   *defensively*   You said you were going to tell them!

ESTELLE   But it isn't any business of yours!

MUM   It is business of ours, though, isn't it, Estelle? Where you go, late at night.

ESTELLE   Late at night! It isn't even dark yet!

MUM   Still, it is getting late. And tonight's not a good night . . .

ESTELLE   Tonight's when it's **on**!

MUM   And anyway, it's silly to get dressed all over again, now you're already in your dressing gown and slippers.

Mum catches sight of Estelle's shifty look.

MUM   Estelle?   *suspiciously*   You **are** undressed, aren't you, Estelle?

Estelle looks away. Mum walks across and unbuttons the dressing gown. Muffy switches her hands from over her ears to over her eyes. Dad looks shocked and horrified.

MUM   Estelle? Estelle! Now listen to me, young lady! You can just go straight upstairs and stuff those horrible clothes in Muffy's dressing-up box, where they belong! If you think your father and I are letting you walk out of this house looking like that, then you are wrong. Dead wrong!

ESTELLE   Look, Mum, I'm not Muffy! I'm me! And I'm not in a nursery. I'm in secondary school! And I'm plenty old enough to go out in the evening!

MUM   Not to one of Alison's parties, you're not!

ESTELLE   Why not?

MUM   Because I've just heard all about them from Chopper's Dad, that's why. And I didn't like what I heard.

He's seen them all, staggering in and out, smoking and swigging from their beercans. And **worse**. And you're not getting mixed up with any of that. You're far too young.

ESTELLE   I'm not too young! I'm not!

DAD   You are while you live under our roof.

ESTELLE   You just don't understand how things are these days. Everyone my age is allowed to smoke! Everyone's allowed to drink! And everyone's allowed to go to Alison's parties! And you can't stop me. I've made arrangements. You have to let me go. You can't treat me like a baby! You can't keep me locked up in this box!

MUM   Box? *dangerously* What box is this, Estelle? I'm looking round for a box. But all I see round me are the ruins of a home. A home your father and I have slaved for years to make a decent, peaceful place for you three to grow up in. And – *Suddenly **Mum** breaks off* Oh, you tell her, George! I simply can't be bothered.

ESTELLE   No! Nobody's going to tell me anything! Not any more! I'm sick of it. Do you understand? Ever since I was old enough to talk, you two have been telling me to listen, and I'm not listening any more. I've had **enough**! Do you understand me? Enough! I'm going upstairs to pack, and then I'm leaving this horrible house for ever! And you'll be sorry!

Estelle slams out. There is a silence.

DAD   Well, you handled that well, didn't you?

MUM   Oh, shut up, George!

DAD   *sighing* Who's going up there after her, then?

MUM   Not me. I've had enough.

DAD   I'm not that keen, either!

MUM   We can't leave things like this, though, can we? **Somebody** certainly has to go.

Dad adjusts an imaginary helmet, and feels for his gun.

DAD   Safety in numbers, Fairway. I'll give you plenty of steady, covering fire.

MUM   No choice, really, have I?

*Sighing, **Mum** moves in front of **Dad**. Together, they make for the door to the stairs, like soldiers expecting an attack.*

*Mum loses her nerve and **Dad** pokes his imaginary gun in her back. Together, they go through the door.*

WILL *admiringly* You see that, Muffy? Do you know what that is? That's solid, grinding courage under fire. And she's not doing it just because she's got his gun stuck in her ribs. Or because we were watching. No, those two are going up there – over the top! – for one reason and one reason only. They believe in what they're doing. They think it's right. They know what sort of horrors face them. And still they're going.

*Will turns to look at **Muffy**.*

WILL I tell you, Muff. You don't see courage like that every day. *He peers at her more closely.* Muff? Muffy?

*Muffy is fast asleep. **Will** pulls a coat over her, and goes to the door. As he opens it, we hear voices from upstairs.*

MUM *off; yelling* . . . become absolutely impossible to live with recently! You dress up in jumble and expect your father and me to let you go out and be seen by the neighbours!

ESTELLE *off; yelling* I think it's my business what I wear!

*Hastily, **Will** shuts the door. Fetching another coat, he snuggles up beside **Muffy** on the floor in the corner, and falls asleep.*

ACT THREE

SCENE ONE

*In the kitchen, two hours later. **Will** mutters in his sleep, reaches for **Muffy** and finds her gone. He staggers blearily to his feet. **Muffy** is at the table, mournfully eating cornflakes. The only light comes from the open fridge door.*

WILL   What's going on? What are you up to?

***Muffy** lifts her bowl.*

WILL   Cornflakes? What **time** is it? Half-past eleven! Why haven't you turned the lights on?

***Will** turns on the overhead light and closes the fridge.*

WILL   Were you worried about waking me? Oh, Muffy! What are you doing feeding your face with cornflakes at this time of night? Were you too hungry to sleep?

***Muffy** nods.*

WILL   For heaven's sake! Your life's getting like mine. But at least I'm allowed to light the gas and use a sharp knife without someone standing over me. Someone your age in this house could very easily starve to death! Is it all over yet? Is it safe to go up to bed?

***Muffy** shakes her head sadly. **Will** opens the door a fraction.*

DAD   *off; yelling*   And you show absolutely no consideration. You ask me 'Can you pick me up at nine?' And if I say yes, it's 'Well, if you're picking me up, can we take Flora home too?' And if I agree to that, then straight away it's 'Can we drop Flora's cello off at her Dad's place?'

39

And after that –

Will shuts the door.

WILL   Poor Stelly. She's had two whole hours of it. Maybe we ought to rescue her.

He opens the door again.

ESTELLE   *off; yelling*   You are so selfish! All you want to do is keep me locked up here, ruining my life, to save yourselves a few miserable droplets of petrol.

Will shuts the door.

WILL   I guess she can look after herself. In fact, she could probably be cloned, and used as a weapon of last resort. 'Bring out your men, or we'll send the Banshee to you!' 'We're coming! Don't do it! We're all coming out!' Spoon up all that milk, Muffy. It's the only thing in that bowl with any goodness in it. Pity your parents are too busy clawing back a few feet of no man's land to feed you properly . . .

Tentatively, he opens the door again.

MUM   *off; yelling*   . . . sullen and cheeky and answering back all the time! Locking yourself in the bathroom for hours on end, and leaving your bits and pieces all over the floor for other people to pick up!

ESTELLE   *off; yelling*   You **never** stop nagging me! You nag me from morning till **night**!

Will shuts the door.

WILL   Frankly, I don't know how Mum and Dad keep it up. I suppose they reckon that if they give in a bit today just because they're worn out, they'll have all that extra ground to make up again tomorrow. It's just trench warfare, really. Except that where William Saffery's unit was fighting for towns and villages along the line, Mum and Dad are defending other things. They're trying not to get forced back on things like drink and drugs and sex, and staying out all night.   *He pulls out his exercise book, and riffles through*   All through my war report, they keep on saying it.   *He reads*   'Can't let her get away with that, George!' 'She's gone too far this time, Heather!' 'We're going to have to make a stand.' Have you finished, Muff?

Do you want an apple? We're war orphans, you and me, Muff. Neglected orphans in the storm of war.

A thunderous sound of footsteps and raised voices coming down the stairs makes **Will** *turn to face the door and* **Muffy** *dive out of sight under the table.*

WILL   And it's coming this way, Muff!

Enter **Mum**, **Dad** *and* **Estelle**, *still arguing.*

DAD   But there's simply no **point** in speaking to you nicely, Estelle, when each time we try to give you a word of sensible advice, you snap our heads off.

ESTELLE   I do not!

Will looks round for **Muffy**. *Suspiciously he lifts the table cloth, stares, then deliberately drops the cloth again.*

MUM   You do, Estelle! In fact, you're hardly ever even civil. Oh, you're all smiles and merry chatter with your friends, and on the phone. But here at home, it's nothing but snarls and unpleasantness.

ESTELLE   It is **not**!

Will is boiling with rage on **Muffy's** *behalf.*

MUM   Oh, yes it is. Ask Will here. Ask your brother what he thinks.

WILL   No! Don't drag me in on this!

MUM   Drag you in on what?

WILL   Your war. Your endless bloody battles. Don't try and make me part of it.

DAD   What's wrong with you all of a sudden?

WILL   What's wrong with me? I'll tell you what's wrong with me!   *He yells*   I've had **enough**!

MUM   *shocked*   Will?

DAD   It's not like you to lose your temper, lad.

WILL   No, maybe it isn't! And maybe that's been my problem all along – that I've been thinking of this great war as nothing to do with me. All these loud voices and slamming doors! I see them as The Other People Show. But that's where I'm **stupid**. Because I know now that **everyone** gets damaged in a war. And I've been just like William Scott Saffery –

DAD   What's the boy on about? Who **is** this William Scott whatsit?

ESTELLE   William Scott **Saffery**. Out of that book he's been reading all the time.

DAD   What book?

WILL   See? You know nothing about me any more! You haven't noticed anything about me for months!

MUM   Will, what has got **into** you?

WILL   I'll tell you what's got into me! The same thing that has got into Muffy!

MUM   Muffy?

WILL   Yes, Muffy. Cowering under the table there!

MUM   Under the table?

WILL   Take a look!

*With a flourish, **Will** lifts the tablecloth. **Muffy** is crouched with her hands over her ears and her eyes tightly shut.*

WILL   See? Battle position! We're all in our battle positions! It's like a bloody war! It just goes on and on! This whole house is a shambles! Nothing but endless rows about Stelly!

ESTELLE   Don't call me Stelly!

***Will** thrusts his face threateningly against **Estelle's**.*

WILL   Shut up! Shut up! **I'm** talking! You can listen to **me!**

***Estelle's** mouth drops open.*

WILL   For months we've put up with your bad temper and your arguments, and the fact that you drain everybody's crystals so dry that Muffy and I scarcely even get a look in, let alone a fair deal!

MUM   Now, Will –

WILL   No, don't 'Now, Will' me! When was the last time anyone found five minutes to give me some lunch money? So long ago, I can't even remember! And why is poor Muffy cowering under the table in the middle of the night? Because she's been eating cornflakes, by herself, in the dark, that's why! You three have been so busy arguing that no one's even thought to feed her properly!

42

MUM Muffy?

WILL So how long is it going on? Go on! Tell us! How much longer? Two years? Three? **Four**? Because I reckon that, like William Saffery's murderous, stupid generals, you three think about everything in this war, except how to bloody well end it!

DAD Listen, son –

WILL No! **You** listen! You listen **hard**. We need some calm and order in this house. I need it. So does Muffy. How can you expect her to speak up with all these rows exploding round her all the time like live shells? We can't go on like this. We need a place to live where people don't have to keep clapping their hands over their ears and diving under tables just to feel a tiny bit safer. Not even safe! I'll tell you what we need. We all need PEACE!

*Will hauls **Muffy** out from under the table and prises her hands off her ears.*

WILL Be brave, Muff. Fight a battle of your own. Tell them you're sick of it. Because you are, aren't you?

Muffy takes a deep breath, and nods.

WILL And if things were a bit more peaceful round here, you might even manage to squeeze a few words out. Isn't that right?

Muffy nods again.

WILL *triumphantly* **See?**

There is silence.

MUM *mortified* Oh, Muffy! I had no idea!

*Mum holds out her arms. **Muffy** rushes into them.*

WILL So? How's it going to be? Are you three going to stop? Is it a cease-fire?

Pause

WILL Mum?

Mum bites her lip, and nods.

WILL Dad?

DAD I'll give it a try, lad. You can depend on that.

WILL   Estelle?

Pause

WILL   Estelle?

ESTELLE   *ungraciously*   Oh, all right! Since it's so important to you two wimpos.

MUM   Estelle –

WILL   **No**, Mum. Leave this to **me**. Try again, Estelle!

ESTELLE   All I said was –

WILL   All you said was – rude, and unfair, and horrible! So try **again**!

ESTELLE   All right. You win. I promise that I'll try. For Muffy's sake.

WILL   No, **not** just for Muffy's sake! For mine, too!

ESTELLE   *irritably*   All **right** then! For yours, too!

WILL   *with elaborate courtesy*   Thank you. Thank you, Estelle. That will do very nicely. For a start.

Dad clicks his heels.

DAD   Jawohl, mein Obergruppenführer!

ESTELLE   What's that?

MUM   He's saying –

Mum salutes Will.

MUM   Yes, **sir**!

ESTELLE   Oh, right. Well, since he's gone bats, I'll humour him.   *Estelle salutes Will as well*   Yes, **sir**!

Muffy salutes.

WILL   *sternly*   Come on, then, Muffy. Spit it out!

MUFFY   *with an effort*   Yes, **sir**!

SCENE TWO

*In the garden, the following morning. **Muffy** is feeding Thumper. **Chopper** and **Will** sit on an upturned wheelbarrow.*

WILL   So then even Muffy does it. 'Yes, sir!' she says. Just like that! Didn't you, Muff?

MUFFY *grinning and saluting* Yes, sir!

WILL And then we all went off to bed.

CHOPPER Amazing! Though, of course, I've always said that your whole family is bats.

WILL And I'd almost begun to believe you. But you're quite wrong, you know. My family isn't really cracking up. William Scott Saffery saw men so badly shattered that nothing and no one would ever put them to rights again. They'd given up. They knew court martial meant a bullet in the head, and still they didn't care. They'd reached the stage where they didn't mind which side of the whole equation was wiped away – the horrors around them, or them. And none of my family's like that. Mum might climb in the back window sometimes, to avoid Estelle. And Muffy hides under tables. But if Estelle's ever going to be allowed out later than helping with Brownies, there's bound to be the odd fight, isn't there?

CHOPPER You've certainly changed your tune a bit since yesterday!

WILL Yes, I suppose I have. I think what happened is, keeping that war report, I suddenly realised how very little of myself was in it.

CHOPPER Well, you're no Banshee!

WILL No, but I'd just gone on, day after day, eating stale carrot sandwiches and such, and never once stood up for what I wanted. I think that's why I kept on reading William Saffery's book. He was like me. He just kept going along with something he didn't believe in, too. Oh, yes. He thought about what he would say to the Big Brass. But Estelle's right. That doesn't take any courage. Anyone can **dream**.

CHOPPER He was your hero, Will! 'Impeccable War Reporter'. That's what you said.

WILL But that's the point. He saw the whole of it for what it was – a stupid, wasteful mess – and he did nothing.

CHOPPER What was he supposed to do? Throw his rifle in the ditch, and be court-martialled himself?

WILL But you've forgotten something.

CHOPPER What?

WILL He was our age.

CHOPPER So?

Will digs out 'The Longest Summer', and finds a page.

WILL So, listen. I must have read it twenty times, and never realised. *He reads* 'I looked around at all these men who had no choice but to stay, and I knew that in my own gift lay my deliverance. All that I had to do was walk back a hundred yards behind the lines and tell them my real age.' So why didn't he, Chopper? It was the longest summer. Don't tell me he didn't think about it all the time. Drop his gun in the mud. Walk back from his position on the line. And, taking care that there were plenty of witnesses standing round him, come out with the magic words: 'I'm not eighteen'.

CHOPPER *thoughtfully* And **still** he didn't do it . . .

WILL No, he didn't do it. Oh, he nursed his comforting little secret like one of Muffy's furry bedtime toys. But still he hung in there, week after murderous week. Until that shell exploded, taking his legs off and saving his life. But how many other young boys he killed in those months, he doesn't say! He came home alive. But look how many didn't!

CHOPPER And he didn't believe in any of it . . .

WILL Not after the first few weeks. And what is so brave about just going along with something you don't even believe in?

CHOPPER When you don't even have to . . .

WILL Just because other men are watching you, perhaps . . .

CHOPPER William Scott Saffery. Impeccable War Reporter –

WILL Or Craven Coward?

CHOPPER Makes you think.

Estelle strolls out, carrying her school bag.

ESTELLE Something that makes Will think? Clear the laboratories! There is a fortune to be made here!

CHOPPER You ought to be more polite about your brother. He's just been sticking up for you.

ESTELLE Really?

CHOPPER That's right. Suddenly, overnight, instead of having you down for a ratty-tempered big-mouth, he reckons you're a good thing, speaking your mind and making your own decisions.

ESTELLE Bit of a turnabout.

CHOPPER That's what I said. Everything's changing round here. Isn't that right, Muffy?

*Muffy nods. **Will** gives a warning cough.*

MUFFY That's right.

CHOPPER Blimey! She speaks! Now I know for sure I've died and gone to the Planet Zog!

Chopper falls backwards in mock astonishment, and comes up clutching a picture book.

CHOPPER Look what I've found.

*Muffy reaches for it. **Will** coughs again.*

MUFFY That's mine.

CHOPPER *reading* 'Beauty and the Beast'. My golly. Have we moved on from 'Rumpelstiltskin' at last? *He reads* 'And love was rewarded, as love always is. For suddenly the Beast rose to his feet, and was a beast no longer. Strong, glorious and true, his virtues shone, like his new face, as brightly as the day.' *Teasing* I reckon this one's about you as well, Estelle. What all your fans here have been waiting for. Really, these old fairy tales do hit the spot.

*Muffy takes the book and hands it to **Will**, stabbing the page with her finger.*

WILL Go on. Make with the words. **Ask** me.

MUFFY Read me the end, please, Will.

WILL But there's only one sentence left after the one Chopper read.

MUFFY Go on. Read it.

WILL If you insist. 'And everything came right at last, in the whole kingdom. And they all lived in happiness and peace.'

Muffy takes the book and hugs it.

WILL   The old fairy-tale ending, eh? It's the best.

A car horn sounds.

CHOPPER   Car pool, Muffy.

Muffy *runs to the gate, hesitates, runs back and hugs* ***Will***, *then* ***Chopper***, *then, after hesitating,* ***Estelle***.

ESTELLE   Do you reckon her car pool would give me a lift to school?

Estelle *starts walking after* ***Muffy***.

CHOPPER   Don't forget to strap yourself safely in your little Snoopy car seat!

Estelle *turns back.*

ESTELLE   I'm warning you, Chopper. Don't push your luck. Not **everything's** changed round here.

Estelle *runs off.*

CHOPPER   It has, though, hasn't it?

Will *is rooting in his lunch bag.*

WILL   *distracted*   Has what?

CHOPPER   Changed. Everything's changed.

Will *draws out a luxurious crusty roll, dripping with exotic fillings.* ***Chopper*** *scavenges those that tumble out.*

CHOPPER   I mean, look at that crusty roll!

WILL   What about it?

CHOPPER   Well, I mean to say, it's like out of one of Muffy's fairy tales. One minute you're a pauper eating scraps. The next, you're noshing through a princely sandwich. What is going on?

Will's *reply is incomprehensible through a mouthful of food.*

CHOPPER   *politely*   Excuse me?

WILL   I said, I've decided to change as well. I'm sick of trailing round after people, whining for money and food. And they're sick of me. And so I've changed the rules.

CHOPPER   Changed the rules?

WILL   Switched the responsibility, really. I've made a deal. Either Dad has to give me a twenty-pound note each time he goes to the bank, and it's up to me to get it changed in time. Or I must add things to the weekly shopping list, so there will always be something to pack.

CHOPPER   Novel. Could work.

WILL   It will work. And, if it doesn't, I'll think of something else.

CHOPPER   Like me and Mum and my late nights out.

WILL   Cunning plan?

CHOPPER   Dead cunning. Mum and I settle between us what time I have to be back. Then she sets the alarm clock for five past and stands it by her door. I creep in dead on time, and switch it off before it wakes her. Then I reset it for the crack of dawn. Hey, presto! I get to see the end of the film or whatever, but Mum doesn't have to lie there worrying in case she falls asleep before it's time to wake up and worry about me.

WILL   What happens if you get home late and the alarm goes off?

CHOPPER   She says that since she's sure I'd never dream of breaking an agreement, naturally she'd assume the worst and phone the police at once. *Darkly* And she would, too. So I've never dared risk it.

WILL   Brilliant! I'll pass that one on to Mum next time Estelle wants to go out to a party.

Estelle comes back.

ESTELLE   *hopefully*   Party?

WILL   What are you doing back again?

ESTELLE   That mean old bag wouldn't take me. Miserable old trout!

CHOPPER   Bad luck, Stelly – whoops! Sorry! Estelle.

ESTELLE   Oh, that's all right, Chopper. You can call me Stelly. Since you're so used to it.

CHOPPER   Oh, ta, Estelle.

Estelle drifts off towards school.

ESTELLE   Bye, then.

CHOPPER   Bye!

WILL   We ought to be going too. It's nearly time.

Chopper is staring after Estelle.

WILL Chopper?

CHOPPER Do you think she meant it?

WILL *sourly* Can't say I'd want to risk it myself.

CHOPPER *wistfully* Did you notice the way she's done her hair this morning?

WILL *aghast* Chopper!

CHOPPER *dreamily* It's not really brown at all, is it, her hair? It's more a sort of **tawny** colour.

WILL Chopper!

*But **Chopper** is already running off after **Estelle**.*

CHOPPER Estelle! Stelly! Wait for me!

***Will** watches' open-mouthed, as his friend leaves.*

WILL Well, there's a turn-up for the book! And what am I supposed to do, left on my tod? Finish the war report? *He pulls out the exercise book* Or go back to reading William Saffery's memoirs? *He takes it from his school bag.* No. Too much has changed round here. That's all behind me now. *He stows them both in Thumper's hutch.* Goodbye, William Scott Saffery. And goodbye, 'Book of the Banshee'. I reckon if Muffy can move on, then I can too!

*Drawing a novel out of his school bag, **Will** strolls off to school, whistling softly and reading.*

STAGING THE PLAY

The Book of the Banshee is a play that is based as much on emotions as on dramatic action. The lives of the Fairway family are violently disrupted by the elder daughter Estelle, until her brother Will proposes a cease-fire.

SET

There are a few potential problems in staging the play. The action takes place mainly in the kitchen of the Fairways' house. On several occasions, one of the characters is supposed to look in the cupboards and fridge, and Estelle's exits will be all the more effective with a door to slam behind her. However, your school may not have the resources or time to build a realistic kitchen set. One solution is to work on mime skills, so that the actors are confident simply miming such actions as looking in a cupboard or slamming a door. A few pieces of furniture, such as a table and chairs, can be used to convey the setting.

Set for a proscenium arch-style stage

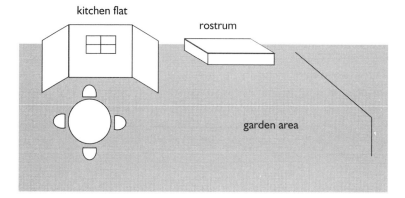

At the beginning of Act Two, Mum is meant to be in bed. You could use chairs pushed together, covered by a blanket or duvet, or a rostrum placed to one side upstage of the kitchen area to suggest the bed in this scene.

SOUND EFFECTS

The sounds of a car and a bus can be used as it is obviously impossible to have actual vehicles in the performance area. Consider sound generally and see if there are points when sound can be used to highlight the action for comic or dramatic effect: for example, an air-raid siren or drumming and marching noises could be used when Mum and Dad set off pretending to be soldiers. Also, think about songs associated with the First World War that Will and Chopper could whistle or sing, such as 'It's a Long Way To Tipperary'.

LIGHTING

Lighting can be used effectively to highlight the different playing areas. Consider how the lighting could change to suggest the garden area. Also, how could non-naturalistic lighting effects be created to exaggerate certain moments for comic effect? For example, a couple of follow-spots in a black-out, plus the sound of air-raid sirens, could be used to reproduce the effect of a bombing raid before, during, or after Mum and Dad's rows with Estelle.

COSTUME

The comedy in the play can be heightened through contrasts: for example, Mum and Dad's change from a crumpled, messy appearance first thing in the morning, into smart business clothes; or Estelle's Cinderella-like transformation when she takes off her dressing gown to reveal her glittery, outrageous party clothes underneath. Will's jumper suffers at the hands of Estelle; it should be seen that she reduces it to an unrecognisable rag.

MAKE-UP

Muffy plays with make-up and the results could be quite disturbing as well as comic. Estelle's make-up should be used to complete her transformation from 13-year-old schoolgirl to vamp.

PROPS

The books belonging to Will and Muffy are important and should be of a size and colour to make them clearly visible throughout the play. The rabbit hutch could be constructed out of cardboard boxes, as it doesn't actually have to hold a live rabbit.

WORK ON AND AROUND THE SCRIPT

Drama

1 The neighbours

Organisation: Work in groups of two or three. You are all neighbours of the Fairways.

Situation: One of you has just seen Mum climbing in through the window.

Opening Line: **FIRST NEIGHBOUR** Do you think she's forgotten her key?

2 Muffy's friend

Organisation: In pairs. One person plays Muffy, the other is her imaginary friend, who may be a character from a fairy tale.

Situation: Muffy is upset because she has just been present at another family row.

Opening Line: **MUFFY** Why do they have to shout all the time?

3 Help for the parents

Organisation: In threes. Two play Mum and Dad, the other is a counsellor.

Situation: Mum and Dad have reached the end of their tether and have decided to visit a counsellor to discuss their problems.

Opening Line: **DAD** I'm not sure whether you can help us.

4 Tableaux

Organisation: In groups representing the Fairway family. Devise and show three 'snapshots' of the family that are set one year before the action of the play, during the action, and a few weeks after it.

Movement

Think about ways to convey age through movement. Muffy in particular has to appear younger and smaller than everyone else. The actor playing Estelle could develop a style of walking and movement that manages to be both slouching and strutting.

Work with masks

The issue of change is important in the play. Make masks using life-size photographs from magazines. It's important to try to use photographs of people, whether they are fashion models or not. Lay the masks out and take turns selecting a mask. After you have put your mask on, look in a mirror, preferably a full-length one, and try to absorb the information that the mask gives you. Look at the way it makes you change your body posture and the movements of your head. Try to produce a voice for the mask and create a monologue telling us about this person and who they are, where they've been and what they've experienced.

Written work

1 Television trailer

Imagine the play is to be shown on television. Select parts of scenes that convey a flavour of the play. Write a spoken narrative that will link the excerpts. The trailer should last no longer than 60 seconds.

2 Review

After you have read the play in the classroom, or seen or performed a production of it, write a review of it for a national newspaper. Alternatively, give a spoken review as if delivering it on television or radio.

3 Cartoons

Select some scenes from the play where Muffy is present and draw them as cartoon strips, complete with speech bubbles for each actor who speaks. Fill thought bubbles for Muffy in each frame with her reactions to and comments on the action.

FROM NOVEL TO PLAYSCRIPT

Not all of the incidents in the novel of *The Book of the Banshee* are included in the play. Read the following extract from the book.

> Quick as a flash, she reached down and pushed my unbuttoned sleeves high up my wrists.
>
> The rash was fierce.
>
> 'That is awful, Will.'
>
> 'It's all right,' I said. 'It isn't bothering me.'
>
> I must be mad. I was in *misery*.
>
> Shrugging, Estelle turned and went back to her table. I looked at Chopper, who was staring at me as if I were

unhinged. Suddenly it was as if all the things I'd learned about myself at the weekend swept back over me in force. This business of changing inside is not quite as simple and straightforward as growing out of your trousers, I can tell you. You can't depend on it. It comes in waves.

Late bloomer I may be; hopeless I'm not.

I stood up and started unbuttoning my shirt.

Chopper was still staring.

'Go on,' I ordered him. 'Take it off.'

'What?'

'Your shirt. Take it off. My skin's very sensitive, and yours isn't. I want to swap shirts.'

He started to argue, but I cut him off.

'Look, Chopper,' I said. 'I can't stand sitting here suffering quietly any longer. So take your shirt off, please.'

Chalky made William Saffery swap boots with him once, for very similar reasons. I thought that was dreadful when I read it first. Now I think I understand.

Chopper could tell I meant it. He stood up. Together we unbuttoned. You don't realize how many people are watching you in a public place, till you do something unusual. I was hardly down to my navel before the shouting and the stamping began. The noise in the lunch hall is always tremendous. This took it over the top. I was a bit embarrassed. After all, I didn't look too fetching, inflamed in great blotchy patches. But Chopper was clearly enjoying the attention, the same way he got a buzz out of it that time we set all the parents off in the school hall.

'Thank you,' he said, bowing to left and right, and flexing his puny muscles. 'Thank you so much. Thank you.'

Amongst all the cries of 'More! More!' and 'Get 'em off!' there were complaints that people at the hatch end couldn't see. Chopper cooperatively climbed on a chair.

'Thank you. You are so kind. Thank you, one and all.'

Miss Sullivan's voice cut through his like a wire through cheese.

'Rupert Murgatroyd Chopperly! Get off that chair at once!'

It isn't fair, using someone's real name as if it's a lethal weapon. A ripple of sympathy ran through the hall. Chopper went pale, and climbed down from the chair. He wouldn't look at her, and she knew better than to push her luck. She just strode out of the hall, and the faint hissing that had greeted her spite grew into a crescendo as she disappeared again through the swing doors.

When I looked back, Flora, Marisa and Estelle were standing in front of us.

'That was *brilliant*, Chopper,' said Flora.

'Your muscles are *huge*,' said Marisa.

(*The Book of the Banshee*, by Anne Fine)

- Why did the author not include this scene in the play? Think of as many reasons as possible.

- Try to dramatise the scene. Write it in play format, complete with stage directions.

- How can you emphasise the comic nature of the scene? Think about the contrast in behaviour between Will and Chopper, and the deflating effect of Miss Sullivan.

THEMES IN AND AROUND THE PLAY

FAMILIES

Discussion

- What are the different roles in the Fairway family?
- Are they an unusual family?
- How would you define a family?

Written work and statistics

Collect some statistics from your own group under the following headings:

1 How many parents work?
2 How many work part-time?
3 How many children are there in each family?
4 How much housework and childcare does each family member do?
5 How much decorating, car maintenance, and gardening does each family member do?

6 How many hours a week does each family member spend on hobbies, not including watching television?

7 How many hours a week does each family member spend watching television?

Try to work these figures out as percentages. For example, Dad does 15 hours of driving and Mum does 5 hours of driving per week. To work out each person's percentage take the following steps:

- First, find the total amount of time spent on each activity by adding together all the figures ($15 + 5 = 20$).
- Then divide 100 by the total ($100 \div 20 = 5$).
- Multiply the answer by the number of hours done by each person ($15 \times 5 = 75$); the answer to this is the percentage. In this example, we have worked out that Dad does 75% of the driving.

Can you draw any conclusions from your data?

Present the group's findings as a social report entitled 'Family and Work in the Nineties'.

Drama

Organisation: In pairs. One plays the child and one the parent.

Situation: The mother has an important job and the child feels neglected.

Opening Line: **DAD** I'm just going to take this cup of tea to your mother.

FOOD

Meals and food reveal a lot in the play; we know that Will is ignored because his lunch is never sorted out, and Will is provoked into taking action by Muffy's midnight meal of cornflakes.

Research and discussion

Consider the ways that food is symbolic of caring and nurturing. Look at different customs and rituals involving food in as many cultures as you can find out about. For example, why do we have wedding cakes? When do we eat special meals and why?

Drama

Create a ritual involving food. The teacher plays the role of the chief minister to the king or queen, and each student brings a piece of food, or a specially prepared meal to the banquet; everyone must present their food, describe it, justify their choice and explain the significance of what they have brought.

POSSESSIONS

Discussion

Possessions are important in the play. Estelle borrows Will's jumper without asking his permission, but Will and Chopper are also guilty of misusing other people's things. What do they do and why?

Drama

1 Favourite thing

Organisation: Initially in pairs. You are good friends.

Situation: One of you shows the other their favourite possession. Discuss why it is so important to you. The other wants to borrow it.

Opening Line: **FIRST FRIEND** I would never part with this.

2 Development

Organisation: The first person has gone, the third person arrives.

Situation: The third person wants to borrow the favourite item from the second person.

Opening Line: **SECOND FRIEND** I'm not sure. S/he didn't say anyone else could borrow it.

3 The friend comes back

Organisation: The second and third friends are joined by the first.

Situation: Something has happened to the favourite item; it has been lost or damaged.

Opening Line: **FIRST FRIEND** Hi! I've come to get the ...

ANGER

Read the following extract from the novel of *The Book of the Banshee* carefully.

In her outrage she leaped on the bed. Her black suede boots were on the coverlet. She danced up and down in her rage.

'You can't do this to me! You can't! I'm not a baby any more. You've got to stop treating me like a child!'

She turned to Dad for help.

'Dad! Stop her! You've got to stop her! Nobody else's mother treats them like this. Nobody's! No one else gets stopped all the time. Other people's parents don't go on and on about how late twelve o'clock is, or things like smoking and drinking. Everyone else will be allowed to go to the discotheque!'

I thought I'd been yelling earlier. But, believe me, till you've heard Estelle yell you've only heard whispering. Estelle's voice can fetch down plaster. She can split walls. Chopper and I aren't joking when we cross our fingers against her for our protection. I tell you, Estelle in a temper is a fiendish sight.

But, just this once, she was outclassed by Mum. I've never seen anything like it. It was astonishing. I had a sudden vision of what Estelle will look like in twenty years. The two seemed so alike. I don't think I've ever really realized before that they share the same black hair, the same green eyes, the same witchy pointing finger. But Mum's still four inches taller. And Mum's got power. Raising herself to her full height, she turned on Estelle a look so withering I practically shrivelled on the spot, just from the fall-out. She looked for all the world like the Bad Queen in 'Snow White' the day the mirror gives her the bad news. The scowl on her face could have cracked glass, the light in her eyes start a forest fire, the steel in her voice cut you down.

The witchy finger pointed deep into Estelle's heart.

'*Nobody* smokes,' declared Mum. '*Nobody* drinks. And *nobody* goes to the discotheque!'

(*The Book of the Banshee*, by Anne Fine)

Written work

In threes, rewrite this scene in the form of a playscript. You could base your dialogue on the play, or use a heightened dramatic language, such as that used in fairy tales or melodrama.

Drama

Now act out the scene in threes; Mum, Estelle and a director, who watches and gives advice to the actors. Try playing the scene in different ways, firstly with both actors speaking very quietly. What effect does this have? Then try it with one being quiet and the other being loud. Can the scene be directed so that it has a climax? How can this be achieved? Experiment with the distance between the actors. What effect does placing one on a higher level than the other have? How does changing the height, distance and focus between the actors alter the impact of the scene?

THE TAMING OF THE SHREW

Baptista, a rich merchant of Padua, has two daughters, Katharina and Bianca. Bianca is beautiful and apparently calm and obedient. She has two suitors, Gremio and Hortensio. Katharina, her elder sister, is a 'shrew', well-known for her jealousy and violent temper.

You may want to find out what happens in the rest of the play and discover why it is called *The Taming of the Shrew*.

Scene: Padua. A room in BAPTISTA's house.
Enter KATHARINA and BIANCA.

Bianca: Good sister, wrong me not, nor wrong yourself,
To make a bondmaid and a slave of me;
That I disdain: but for these other gawds,
Unbind my hands, I'll pull them off myself,
Yea, all my raiment, to my petticoat;
Or what you will command me will I do,
So well I know my duty to my elders.

Katharina: Of all thy suitors, here I charge thee, tell
Whom thou lov'st best: see thou dissemble not.

Bianca: Believe me, sister, of all the men alive
I never yet beheld that special face
Which I could fancy more than any other.

Katharina: Minion, thou liest. Is't not Hortensio?

Bianca: If you affect him, sister, here I swear
I'll plead for you myself, but you shall have him.

Katharina: O! then, belike, you fancy riches more:
You will have Gremio to keep you fair.

Bianca: Is it for him you do envy me so?
Nay, then you jest; and now I well perceive
You have but jested with me all this while:
I prithee, sister Kate, untie my hands.

Katharina: If that be jest, then all the rest was so.

Strikes her. Enter BAPTISTA.

Baptista: Why, how now, dame! whence grows this insolence?
Bianca, stand aside. Poor girl, she weeps.
Go ply thy needle; meddle not with her.
For shame, thou hilding of a devilish spirit,
Why dost thou wrong her that did ne'er wrong thee?
When did she cross thee with a bitter word?

Katharina: Her silence flouts me, and I'll be reveng'd.

Flies after BIANCA.

Baptista: What! in my sight? Bianca, get thee in.

Exit BIANCA.

Katharina: What! will you not suffer me? Nay, now I see
She is your treasure, she must have a husband;
I must dance bare-foot on her wedding-day,
And, for your love to her, lead apes in hell.

```
*************************************************
* Talk not to me: I will go sit and weep        *
* Till I can find occasion of revenge.          *
*                                               *
*                   Exit.                       *
*                                               *
* Baptista: Was ever gentleman thus griev'd as I? *
*************************************************
```
(*The Taming of the Shrew*, Act Two, Scene One,
by William Shakespeare)

Drama

1 Work in a group of four. Three of you take on the roles of Bianca, Katharina and Baptista. The fourth member of the group becomes director.

Read the scene carefully. Feelings are at a high pitch throughout. Discuss the motivation of each character and consider how the scene might be presented in order to convey these contrasting emotions successfully, paying particular attention to voice and movement.

2 To create the motivation for the above scene, you could, in the same groups, improvise the scene beforehand that leads into it. Why do you think Katharina was so angry with Bianca that she actually tied her hands? You might consider the following alternatives, or invent your own:
  • Bianca has been teasing Katharina about how old she is.
  • Bianca has been boasting about the number of boyfriends she has.
  • Bianca has rubbed it in that she is her father's favourite.

3 Baptista could be played as either the mother or the father of Katharina and Bianca. Create a scene where the parent is confiding in a friend about the problems between the daughters.

Written work

1 Write an extract from Katharina's diary that shows us how she really feels.

2 Write a letter from Bianca to a friend describing life with Katharina.

TAKING CONTROL

Drama

Organisation: Two people start improvising a scene. When the teacher claps their hands, another person walks into the scene and changes it completely. Introduce more and more new people, each of whom changes the scene, until the entire group is involved.

Opening Line: You could use the following opening line if you want: **FIRST PERSON** What are you doing here?

UNNATURAL MOTHERS

Discussion

1 In the following extract from *Hideous Kinky*, Esther Freud's mother has taken 5-year-old Esther and 7-year-old Bea to North Africa. Their father does not live with them and their mother has a hippie lifestyle, despite the presence of her young daughters.

> Mum began to pray again, facing east on her mat. She practised yoga positions, including the lotus, and talked about a new adventure. The more restless she became the more Pedro enthused about spending the whole summer at Sid Zouin. Bea, having worked through to the last lesson in her book, said she should really be getting back to school, preferably in England. I thought about Bilal searching for us, wandering through the cafés, standing in the empty rooms of the Hotel Moulay Idriss. I practised tightrope walking on the garden wall, threw myself into handstands that were meant to turn into backflips but never did, and tried to pluck up the courage to extinguish the burning head of a match in my open mouth.
>
> Bea and I sat in the taxi and waited for Mum and Pedro to say goodbye. They stood together in the arched doorway of the garden wall and held hands.

'Come on,' we whined at intervals.

Scott and Jeannie didn't come to see us off. Jeannie hadn't forgiven Mum for refusing to listen to her offers of advice. 'That language will get them into trouble,' she had warned and, 'Children need discipline.'

'I had plenty of discipline,' Mum said, 'and it didn't do me any good.'

Pedro stood in the street and watched our car as it drove away. His face looked sad. Mum put her hand out of the side window and waved but she didn't turn round.

As soon as Pedro was out of sight, she began to explain her plan: 'We'll stay in Marrakech for a few nights, wait for some money to arrive and then we're off to Algiers to visit the Zaouia.'

'What about school?' Bea said.

'And what about Bilal?'

'If Bilal's in Marrakech,' Mum assured me, 'we'll be sure to find him.'

'The Gnaoua might know, or the Fool,' I suggested, 'or the Nappy Ladies at the hotel.'

(*Hideous Kinky*, by Esther Freud)

- Who do you think Pedro is?
- Why does Jeannie disapprove?
- Why does Mum say that discipline did her no good?
- Why do you think Bea is concerned about school?
- Do you think Mum is a 'good' mother?
- What are Esther's feelings throughout the extract?

2 Read the following list of key characteristics of the basically healthy family.

> • An essentially positive approach to life and other people, often manifested as a high level of humour, fun and enjoyment.
> • A strong commitment and sense of involvement, and an unusual degree of closeness and intimacy.
> • A capacity for individual members to be independent, separate and happy on their own.
> •Efficient communication between family members with open, frank and clear conversations about everything.
> • Firm control of family activity by the parents, after consultation with all involved, and as far as possible the accommodation of all points of view.
> • An equal-power coalition between a mother and father who can resolve issues easily and amicably.
> • An ability to cope with change and loss, even including the death of loved ones.

(from *The Children We Deserve*, by Rosalind Miles;
extract based on *Families and How to Survive Them*,
by Robin Skynner and John Cleese)

• Do you think Esther's family have the characteristics listed above?

• Do the Fairways have them? Compare the Fairway family at the start and at the end of the play.

GROWING UP

Discussion

> Chopper ... embarked on a precis of his most recent reading.
> 'In this book about the awkward adolescent', he told me, 'It says the childhood personality has to break down, so that a new one can grow.'

(*The Book of the Banshee*, by Anne Fine)

- What makes a teenager turn into a grown-up?
- When does it happen?
- How can you tell it has happened?

Written work

Think about the qualities that grown-ups are meant to have. Choose someone you know whom, regardless of their age, you consider to be a grown-up. Write a profile of them explaining why you think they are 'grown-up'.

FAIRY TALES

Written work

Muffy goes into a world of fairy tales as a way of avoiding conflicts within her family. Write the story of the Fairways as if they were in a fairy tale for young children.

Drama

In small groups, pick a fairy tale and read it carefully. What is the message concealed in the story? Turn it into a modern-day story and act it out to the rest of the group. Discuss whether it worked as a modern tale, and why.

WAR

Discussion

The images and language of war are used to describe the relationships within the Fairway family. Why has the author chosen to do this? Does it work? What other parallels or comparisons could have been used instead?

THE FIRST WORLD WAR

'Since August 1914 ... we've got about as far as an asthmatic ant carrying some heavy shopping.'

(Captain Blackadder, *Blackadder Goes Forth*,
by Richard Curtis and Ben Elton, BBC Television)

The facts
- The First World War is also known as the Great War because of the huge loss of human life on both sides; almost an entire generation was wiped out or damaged, and no family escaped loss.
- On 1st July 1916 at the Somme, there were 60,000 British casualties. The battle was presented as a victory.
- Between July and November 1916 the British sustained around 420,000 casualties for an advance of 6 miles.

Research and written work

1 Find out as much as you can about the First World War.
Write William Scott Saffery's diary for the first week of the
war, starting just before he joins up. Then write entries
covering his last few days in the war, including being
injured and invalided out.

Drama

1 War poetry

■ IN FLANDERS FIELDS

In Flanders fields the poppies blow
Between the crosses, row on row
  That mark our place; and in the sky
  The larks, still bravely singing, fly
Scarce heard amid the guns below.

We are the Dead. Short days ago
We lived, felt dawn, saw sunset glow,
  Loved and were loved, and now we lie
    In Flanders fields.

Take up our quarrel with the foe:
To you from failing hands we throw
  The torch; be yours to hold it high.
  If ye break faith with us who die
We shall not sleep, though poppies grow
    In Flanders fields.

John McCrae, 1872-1918

- Try this poem as a choral piece. Decide how to divide it up
  for maximum effect.
- Work out a dance drama to accompany the speaking and/or
  singing of the poem.

2 First World War family

Organisation: Look at the picture. Try to imagine the family background of William Saffery. In small groups, decide who will be his mother, father, brother(s), and/or sister(s). To start you off, you could model it on Will Fairway's family. What sort of people are they? Do they all feel the same way about the war? Think about when they lived. Could children express what they felt to their parents? Were women expected to have opinions about things like war?

Situation: The family are at tea. Father is reading the paper.

Opening Line: **FATHER** Look at what the damn Germans are up to now.

3 Hopes and dreams

Create a monologue for each member of William Saffery's family, which tells us a bit about their character. Have them talk about their feelings when they discovered that Will had run away to join up.

4 Invalided out

Organisation: Re-form into your family groups.

Situation: Will arrives home from the war. How do you react to his arrival? What do you ask him about the war and his reasons for joining up? What are your feelings and emotions?

5 Development

Organisation: Split the family into smaller groups. Have the father, brothers and Will overhear the following scene.

Situation: Will's sister has decided to join the V.A.D. (Voluntary Aid Detachment). She is telling her mother of her decision. Other sisters may be present and either decide to join, or to dissuade her.

Opening Line: **SISTER** Since Will came back, I've been feeling so useless. You don't need me here and I know I could do some good abroad, as a nurse.

Follow-Up: What is the reaction of her family? Develop some more scenes. Perhaps Will can talk to her and try to describe the horror of war.

IN HOSPITAL

The following extract recounts some memories of a V.A.D. nurse who worked in a field hospital at the front.

I used to hate it if they died when I was on night duty, because then you had to lay them out yourself. But if they died during the day, the orderlies always did that. My first night duty was on this very heavy ward. There was one man, he'd been a fisherman in civil life and he had dreadful wounds, internal wounds, all fastened up with tubes that ran into a bucket underneath his bed. His bed was up against the door of the marquee, because anyone who was likely to die was always put there so that they could be taken out without fuss and depressing the rest of the wounded. I was terrified that he would die when I was on night duty, and the first thing I used to ask the day nurse when I went on was, 'Is the fisherman still alive?' She said he was, but he was very near death. But as soon as I went in and got into the marquee he called me and said, 'Sister, can you give me the drink you gave me last night?' I'd given him some port warmed with a bit of water and sugar and he wanted it again. I gave him the drink and I sat with him.

A little while before he died he opened his eyes and said, 'You've been an angel to me.' It made me feel absolutely dreadful. I thought, 'Thank goodness he doesn't know what I've been thinking, just hoping all the time that he wouldn't die when I was on duty.' But he died that night. The night superintendent came in. She was an elderly Scotswoman, and very kind. She said, 'I'll do the laying out and you hold the lantern for me.' So we put the screens round and started to lay out this poor man, ready for the orderlies to take him away. Of course, the rest of the ward was in darkness and the men were sleeping, and there was only a dim light and us behind the screens in this shadowy corner with the poor, dead soldier. Half-way through, as we turned the body over, Sister looked at me and shook her head. 'We do have to do some things, don't we!' she said.

(Kitty Kenyon, V.A.D., No. 4 General Hospital, Camiers)

Discussion

- Why did the nurse hate laying out the bodies?
- What do you think a hospital like this would have been like?

Written work

Imagine you are the dying soldier. Write a letter home as if it may be your last.

Drama

1 Create a scene based on the information contained in the extract. Work in fours; three actors and a director. How can you make it as effective and moving as possible?
2 Develop a play out of all the material and scenes you have worked on in this section on the First World War. You could use Will's diary entries, and war poems or songs to link the scenes.

WAR TODAY

Survivors from a concentration camp in former Yugoslavia

Discussion

What do we know about war today? What images do we
remember? What are we shown on television? How are
things presented to justify wars? What sort of propaganda
are we subjected to? Why is propaganda used?

Written work

Collect a week's worth of cuttings from newspapers about the
various wars that are currently raging. In pairs, sort out the
information, or get background material from the library and
compile your own report from a war-torn area. Imagine
yourself actually there and how it must be. Deliver your
report as a television or radio broadcast, or write it up as a
newspaper report.

NUCLEAR WAR

■ 'APPENDIX IV
REQUIREMENTS IN THE SHELTER

> Clothing
> Cooking equipment
> Food
> Furniture
> Hygiene
> Lighting
> Medical
> Shrouds'

What

> 'Shrouds.
> Several large, strong black plastic bags
> and a reel of 2-inch, or wider, adhesive tape
> can make adequate airtight containers for deceased
> persons until the situation permits burial.'

No I will not put my lovely wife into a large strong black
    plastic bag
No I will not put my lovely children into large strong black
    plastic bags
No I will not put my lovely dog or my lovely cats into large
    strong black plastic bags
I will embrace them all until I am filled with their
    radiation
Then I will carry them, one by one,
Through the black landscape
And lay them gently at the concrete door
Of the concrete block
Where the colonels
And the chief detectives
And the MPs
And the Regional Commissioners
Are biding their time

And then I will lie down with my wife and children
And my dog and cats

And we will wait for the door to open.

Adrian Mitchell

Many young people are concerned about the threat of nuclear war. Looking at the above poem, examine the way in which the writer conveys his feelings about this threat. What action does he intend to take? How does the black humour work effectively in this poem?

FALKLANDS WAR

Read the following extract.

> On Saturday night, 3 April 1982, I was in Portsmouth with British squaddies and sailors drinking last pints, squeezing girls before embarking for the Falkland Islands. They hadn't seen their country carved up by greed-crazed politicians bent on graft and bribery, nor learned how to talk aid agency personnel into relinquishing a few sacks of grain, nor been to party indoctrination school, nor fought in a war. They knew more about the dole, Paddy-bashing and nuclear games in NATO. They were open, frank and a bit concerned. They were also kids.
>
> Soon they learned a few cold and windswept truths in the South Atlantic. Much of the fighting in the Falklands was a bloody close match. There was little doubt that Britain would win. But at what cost? A lot of men who returned are more genuinely confident now. They're also more sober, the realisation coming to them under fire that the "Argies" aren't Spanish-speaking idiots, that most of the Argentine forces had good weapons, adequate clothing, some fine air support and at times fought fiercely and well. Without American Sidewinder missiles the air war could have been very different. Without American satellite communications British tactics could well have floundered. It seems as if General Galtieri's forces have been the historic instrument to drive home the high price of keeping Britain's already much diminished sovereignty overseas intact. Newsstand thrillers and the "Gotcha!" press hadn't prepared squaddies for that.
>
> Now they know. The question today is whether their parents and the rest of the British public will ever find out.
>
> Behind the razzamataz, bunting and drum thumping victory speeches the Falklands affair was an unedifying sight. The British government had been caught with its

pants down, and before they were hoiked up again a couple of billion pounds had been dumped into the South Atlantic and several hundred men were dead.

Before that happens again it might be a good idea if several more journalists and their editors quietly ditched their tired lies and fawning mimicry. They don't have to go the whole hog and begin prowling the offices of Third World revolutionary movements, interviewing men on the run in chintzy bed-and-breakfast hotels, working the other side of the street as it's called. But they might just once give the Foreign Office a miss, and just once skip those off-the-record briefings and chats with their school chums. They might just try to think for themselves. Isn't that, after all, what independence of the press is all about?

(*Hack*, by Ed Harriman)

- What are the writer's feelings about the Falklands War?
- How does he express them?
- What is his central argument?
- Look at the language and phrases that the writer uses. Why are these effective?

PROTESTORS

Discussion

Men who either refused to bow to peer pressure and join up, or who refused their draft, were known as Conscientious Objectors, or 'Conchies'. They were often insulted and given white feathers, a sign of cowardice, by squads of patriotic women. During the Vietnam War, young men avoiding their call-up papers were known as 'draft dodgers'.

- Estelle criticises William Saffery for obeying orders. Do you agree with her views?
- Under what circumstances should people fight?
- Should people be forced to join the army in times of war?
- Who should make the decision to start or join a war?

THERE ARE
THREE
TYPES OF MEN

Those who hear
the call and obey

Those who delay

And — The Others

TO WHICH DO
YOU BELONG?

Research and discussion

What protest groups exist today that defy the law? Collect
information about Greenpeace, C.N.D., animal rights
activists, roadway protestors, and so on.

- What are the positive and negative aspects of each group?
- How do they get their message across?
- Are their actions and behaviour right?
- What have they achieved?

Drama

1 In small groups, set up a protest group. Decide on your
   name and the aims of your group. How would you achieve
   them? How would you get maximum publicity for the
   group? Write your manifesto and some advertisements to
   recruit people to your cause.

2 Plan a campaign of action.

3 Your plan is discovered by a reporter, who prints the story. Other people outside the group start to react to it as a result; create their roles. They may include police, parents, friends outside the group, and politicians.

4 Collect impressions about the protest group from those inside and outside the group. What overall image does it have? Is it a successful group? What are the problems? How can these be solved? What action should the group take next?

SOCIAL ISSUES

Language used about women

> **banshee** *n.* (in Irish folklore) a female spirit whose wailing
> warns of impending death. [C18: from Irish Gaelic *bean sídhe*,
> literally: woman of the fairy mound]

(Collins English Dictionary)

Discussion

Read the following poem.

■ THE BANSHEE

> *what*
> *a nightmare strangeness life is*
> *at death point*
>   Marina Tsvetaeva

1.
White – like the full moon
outside my window
you waken me –
and I climb towards you
as if you were
my way out –
female voice
rising and falling
in hypnotic
bittersweet waves

You pace the dark hills
around this house
crying the tears
I feel too numb
to cry –

82

and I welcome you,
wanting to die

You point the way
to my house –
and I never felt
more alive,
tender towards
everyone.
Why do you love me?
Is it because
you alone hear
my outrageous
thoughts?

Three shrieks
make the valley
echo.
Tree-roots tremble
the sky shakes
I shake.
Three more shrieks
loud enough
to deafen anyone –
yet only I hear you
quieten again,
your lonely sound
calling me away

Your eyes are red
with centuries
of crying.
Mine are tired
and dry
from inward lament.
Both of us
so thin the wind
could break us.
You shiver violently
from cold and grief.
I am shaken
with longing
for someone
who doesn't exist

Are you the spirit
of a silent woman
who walked
the hills
above her village?
Sad ancestor
urging me
to say the words
that set us free

Susan Connolly

- What are the writer's feelings about the banshee? Is she afraid of her?
- What does the banshee do for the writer? What are the words that 'set us free'?

Written work

Make two lists, one of all the animal names that are applied to women (e.g. cow), and one of animal names that are applied to men (e.g. stallion). In what ways are the two lists different?

Now make a list of all the words that could be used to describe Estelle. Divide the list into words that describe 'good' qualities and those that describe 'bad' qualities. Now imagine that the words are being applied to a boy. Which words change to become either 'good' or 'bad' when they are applied to a boy, and why?

Discussion

Read the following report.

Teachers' Attitudes

Recently, the Department of Education at the University of Surrey carried out a survey. A group of teachers was given a student's report. The student was unruly and inattentive, yet managed to get good marks in some, but not all, subjects. Half of the teachers were told that the student was called 'John Smith' and the other half were told that the student's name was 'Joan Smith'. The teachers with 'John's' report decided he was 'possibly very bright' with 'good career prospects'. Many of his problems were seen as his teachers' fault. 'Joan', on the other hand, was dismissed as a drop-out with no intellectual potential.

Why was 'Joan' labelled a failure? Why did the teachers see 'John' as having such potential? Does the same situation exist in your school? Are boys treated differently in class? Are they disruptive in the way that Estelle complains of in her school? Do the boys think they need more attention, and why? Why do boys and girls behave so differently? Do girls get a fair deal in school and in work?

EDUCATION

In the play, Estelle states that school is useless.

Discussion

Set up a debate. Two debaters defend the motion 'This house believes in education' and two debaters oppose it. Present your speeches and get the audience to vote on which are the best.

What can you learn from the debate? What skills and knowledge do you want to acquire? How should you learn them and when? What would you like to have in place of formal education?

TEENAGERS

Discussion and written work

1   Write an article for your local paper entitled 'Teenagers in Britain today'.

2   In a group, discuss which soap or sitcom characters remind you of Estelle. How are they presented? (Think about Harry Enfield's Kid Brother, Darlene in *Roseanne*, or Bianca in *Eastenders*, for example.) Write profiles of the characters you have discussed.

3   Make two lists side by side, one of the things that annoy your parents most about you, and one of what annoys you about them. Share your lists with the rest of the group. What are the common themes?

4   Make up a magazine advice page and contribute letters to the page about family problems based on the list. Try to answer the letters with advice and common sense. Use a computer to make the page look as much like a magazine as possible.

Drama

1 The row

Organisation: In threes. Two play parents and one is the teenage son or daughter.

Situation: The teenager has come in late.

Opening Line: **PARENT** What time do you call this, young man/woman?

2 The court room

Either use the above example, or one from the list of annoying things you have drawn up. Try to work out a solution between you. Failing that, set up a teenagers' court, where an impartial judge and a jury made up of the rest of the group will hear both sides of the argument. How does this change the approach to the problem? Each jury member should suggest a solution, perhaps along the line that Chopper tells us he has worked out with his mother. The judge will ask everyone to vote for the best way to solve the problem.

3 Television programme

Prepare a script for a television programme about teenagers in Britain today. What are their biggest problems? What is the image of teenagers in the media? Decide how you would put the programme together. Role-play being parents, teenagers, social workers, teachers, police and the documentary makers. Draw up interview questions and try to create a balanced view.

FURTHER READING

The Monocled Mutineer, by William Allison and John Fairley (Hutchinson)
Testament of Youth, by Vera Brittain (Virago)
Tales of the Banshee, by Patrick Byrne (Mercia Press)
The Mill on the Floss, by George Eliot (Penguin)
Banshee: The Irish Supernatural Death Messenger, by Patricia Lysaght (Glendale Press)
War Poems, by Christopher Martin (Collins Educational)
The Catcher In The Rye, by J. D. Salinger (Penguin)
The Growing Pains of Adrian Mole, by Sue Townsend (Mandarin)